John W. De Peyster

Bothwell

James Hepburn, fourth earl of Bothwell, third husband of Mary, queen of

Scots - An historical drama

John W. De Peyster

Bothwell
James Hepburn, fourth earl of Bothwell, third husband of Mary, queen of Scots - An historical drama

ISBN/EAN: 9783337325619

Printed in Europe, USA, Canada, Australia, Japan

Cover: Foto ©Andreas Hilbeck / pixelio.de

More available books at **www.hansebooks.com**

BOTHWELL:

(JAMES HEPBURN, FOURTH EARL OF BOTHWELL, THIRD HUSBAND
OF MARY, QUEEN OF SCOTS.)

𝔄n 𝔥istorical Drama.

"Not myself, but the word that in life I have spoken;
Not myself, but the deed that in life I have done;
Shall pass on to ages, all about me forgotten,
Save the truth I have spoken, the deed I have done."
H. BONAR.

BY

 JOHN WATTS DE PEYSTER.

New York:

CHARLES H. LUDWIG, PRINTER, 10 & 12 READE STREET.

1884.

BOTHWELL:

AN HISTORICAL DRAMA.

INTRODUCTION.

" It is difficult to estimate facts delivered under circumstances which deprive the testimony of all moral value ; when falsehood is not an accident, but a property of the speaker's character, and is not the error of a moment or the crime of an individual; but an organic system." *"Nimrod,"* II., 494 ; HIGGIN'S *"Anacalypsis,"* II., 42.

Quite a library of works had been already collected and consulted and compared with others almost as numerous in public libraries, before the writer gave to the world the first of his Trilogy, entitled "Mary Queen of Scots : A Study." After that was published, he found that the subject had enlisted the pens of able men all over Europe, whose works were unknown in this country and some of them even in England and Scotland, except to a very small number whose studies led in this particular direction. Orders were immediately sent out to different book-centres and a number of rare as well as recent treatises rewarded the search.

The second of the Trilogy, "James Hepburn, Earl of Bothwell : A Vindication," was a work of much less labor than the first. Shortly after this appeared, still farther research revealed new authorities ; and after an examination, analysis and comparison, even more elaborate than the two previous ones, appeared the Third of the Trilogy : "An Inquiry into the Career and Character of Mary Stuart (*"Crux Criticorum"*), (" The puzzle of critics "), and a Justification of Bothwell. (*"Audire est operæ Pretium."*) (" What is herein disclosed is worthy of attention.") Scarcely had this been published when a number of catalogues, containing the names of still further authorities. which had escaped previous inquests, were transmitted from various

friends, collectors, librarians and students ; and, as the result of all
this, the writer's private library on Mary Stuart, which at first required only one large case, would now fill several.

At Edinburgh, Scotland, 1888, was published a very interesting
work, by the Reverend Joseph Stevenson, S. J. (Jesuit), entitled
" The History of Mary Stuart, from the Murder of Rizzio until her
Flight into England. By Claude Nau, her secretary. Now first printed
from the original manuscripts, with illustrative papers from the secret
archives of the Vatican and other collections in Rome."

Doubtless, besides this manuscript of Nau, others of equal importance, perhaps, lie hidden among the uncollated documents of some of
the public libraries in Rome, Spain, Paris, England and Scotland, or
among the family archives of prominent Scottish families, whose an-
cestors were connected with events transpiring during the reign of
Mary Stuart. Such documents may also exist in the collections left
by the descendants of the envoys or agents sent over by the French
Government to the Court of Mary. Careful search might even dis-
cover something contemporary among the papers left behind by the different representatives of England, in Scotland, between the dates of
the birth of Mary and the accession of James, her son, to the crowns
of Scotland and England. There should be documents of the highest
importance relating to Bothwell in the appropriate public depositories
at Copenhagen or some of the Royal Residences—although so many
of the latter have been destroyed by fire that it would be very easy to
account for the absence of such authorities. Nor should the possibility
of solving problems of the greatest interest. now involved in mystery,
in regard to the last years of Bothwell, be abandoned until the last
scrap of parchment or paper preserved by the families of the nobility
of Scania, has been scrutinized with extreme care. Something might
even be found at Stockholm or Upsala, whither so many old collections
gradually found their way ; or at Skokloster, that castle-mine"'or
bonanza of the secrets and curiosities of the past, since the fingers of
the Wrangels seem to have been like those of Jack Sheppard, perfect
" lime twigs," to which everything remarkable that came in contact
with them was almost sure to adhere.

The names of the works obtained, as well as of those examined (if the latter are not too numerous), will be appended to complete the "List of Authorities," published at pages 209, 210, 211, of Number Three of the Trilogy previously referred to.

The fact is, that the investigation of the careers and characters of Mary Stuart and of Bothwell, which at first was an amusement or an occupation, has become almost a passion ; because the deeper that the writer has plunged into historical research, the more convincing has become the proof that in these, as in very many other cases, political, personal and religious prejudices and partialities, falsehood, not truth, have painted the portraits of the unfortunate Queen, and the still more unfortunate Bothwell, her third husband—the latter the most unhappy in life as well as in death,—seeing that Mary has found a multitude of defenders ; whereas those who champion her cause vie with her worst enemies in striving to blacken the character of Bothwell ; seeming to be convinced within themselves that one among the surest methods to rehabilitate her character is to demonstrate that she was the victim of a villain, Bothwell ; whereas he, in fact, was victim of her, as well as of her bastard brother, the Earl of Murray, finally Regent of Scotland— than whom a falser man and in many respects a greater political villain never lived : except in so far that, in a period of barbarism and sensuality, he found sufficient employment in accomplishing the ruin of Mary, Bothwell, Darnley, in fact whoever stood in his way ; to let the the three German W's, "*Wein, Weibern und Wurfel,*"—Wine or wassail, women and gambling ; especially women, as paramours, of whom to his sorrow his father, James V., was so fond, severely alone.

Among the many curious books on this subject obtained from Germany, is one entitled "*Maria, Königin von Schottland,* von Friedrich Gentz. Braunschweig, 1799."

It is a diminutive quarto and presents, together with a certainly unique portrait, two other engravings, one of the Murder of Rizzio, and the other of Mary taking leave of her servants before execution ;—but the most curious feature of it is, that few of the pages are of equal size—some are quarto shape, some duodecimo, and some even more irregular in shape.

Another even more curious work, entitled "*La Covr Sainte Dv. R. Pere Nicolas Cavssin de la compagnie de Iesvs. Mise en vn Bel*

Ordre. Avec vne notable augmentation des Vies des personnes illus-
tres de la Cour, taut du vieil que du nouveau Testament. Et augmen-
tée en cette derniere Edition de la vie de l'Autheur et de diuerses
Histoires. [Two volumes in one. Folio, large.] A Paris, chez Iean.
Dv. Bray, rue Sainte Iaques, aux Espics meurs et au Chapelier (?)
M.DC.LIII. avec privilege, et approbation."

The likeness of Mary Stuart, Queen of Scots, attached to this book
very much resembles a number in the possession of the writer (who
has collected perhaps a hundred different engravings, &c.), and presents an additional proof that Mary's fascination lay more in her
"marvelous agreableness," her grace, accomplishments, language, manner and expression, than in the mere physical beauties of form, face
and features, by which the vast majorities of the male sex are completely carried away.

Without putting much faith in the statements of a member of the
Society of Jesus — a Jesuit; nevertheless, on the principle, that the
devil may quote Scripture appositely — Father Caussin is not far
out of the way in his estimate of the Earl of Murray. He says (II.
308), "that he was a dangerous and dissolute man." If by "dissolute" he means a man whose ambition knew no restraint of morals,
he is perfectly correct, and especially when he adds that Murray was
a mere instrument in the hands of Queen Elizabeth, and scattered the
seeds that germinated and produced a harvest of tragedies. After
having filled his lungs with breath of a furious and turbulent ambition,
which was breathed into them by Knox, the patriarch of the Scottish
Reformers, Murray never ceased to assume the quality of Regent and
aspire to the authority of King without sparing any detestable wickedness by which he could arrive at the goal of his desires. To avert
Mary's marriage with a foreign prince, which might have buttressed
her own with a sufficient power to assert her authority, he managed
to throw her into the arms of Darnley, hoping thereby to insure the
real administration to himself. Finding that, in consequence of Mary's
passion for her boy-husband, he, Murray, was likely to fail of his object, he determined to get rid of the latter. Murray possessed at the
Court of Scotland an agent in the Earl of Morton, who was nothing
more than his *Alter Ego.* To him he confided the commission of throw-

ing the apple of discord into the marriage-bed of the King and Queen. This Morton accomplished with incredible artifice, so that this master-mechanic of iniquity was able to kindle two furnaces with the same breath, unceasingly firing the heart of the Queen with proofs of her husband's miserable conduct, and at the same time lighting in the bosom of the latter ambitious aspirations which were the more hateful in that they were the offspring of an ingratitude which was based at once on a detestable character and cowardice.

In all this the Jesuit ignores the latent influence of Mary's long-seated prediliction for the Earl of Bothwell, which like the etherial circulation of the impalpable force-imparting fluid through the tubes of the nerves, is just as necessary to the vitality of man as the perceptible ebb and flow of the visible red blood, which is life itself. Murray's influence through various agencies, of whom Morton was the chief, brought about the murder of Rizzio—a blow which was aimed as much at Mary and the child in her womb, afterwards James VI., as at the miserable musician, minister of state and papal emissary, who was stabbed and almost slain at the very feet of the Queen.

The miserable prince whom jealousy had impelled to the murder of the favorite, was now the next obstacle which stood in Murray's path. Mary's love for Bothwell and his life-long love for her, were to be converted into elements of destruction for both. Murray and his co-conspirators felt that if Bothwell and the Queen could be implicated in the murder of Darnley, and then be mutually guilty of adultery and assassination, and finally united in marriage, public opinion could be so excited against them that Bothwell would be driven from the kingdom and ruined irremediably, Mary thrust from her throne, blasted in character, and the whole authority and its advantages remain at the disposal of Murray and his co-partners in iniquity. The story of what followed reads as if the successive results were simply a rehearsal of the details of the plan.

The good Jesuit tells the story, in some respects, sufficiently well that it will be interesting simply to translate some of the passages of his almost obsolete French. "Some time after the death of the king [Darnley], Bothwell, who was one of the powerful noblemen in Scotland, dared to seek the Queen in marriage, since the Earl of Mur-

ray had promised that, as a recompense of his crime." [Putting Darnley out of the way.]   *   *   *

In order to reconcile Mary to the match with a man who " was sus-
pected of so detestable a deed—even if he was innocent, besides being
already married ; the bastard, Murray, and the other conspirators who
had undertaken this affair with such obstinate resolution, managed to
have the criminal acquitted by judges who belonged to their faction ;
and furthermore arranged matters, so as to satisfy the Queen as to the
removal of the other obstacle, a living wife."   *   *   *   Father
Caussin then proceeds to describe how this Philistine [Bothwell] adored
this lovely arch of alliance, the willing captive of his bow and spear
at Almond Bridge.

" It was on this occasion that the Earl of Murray, who had withdrawn a little, so as to avoid any suspicion of being concerned in the
murder of Darnley, returned to court and encouraged the suit of the
King's murderer, rewarding him with the conquest of the most beautiful Queen in the world, in full payment of what he had done. Murray
did not cease to press Mary to accept Bothwell as her husband, urging
upon her the public avowal of the Earl's innocence, the splendor of
his house, his courageous exploits and the proofs of his fidelity, all of
which rendered him worthy of her love. He added that being alone,
and without support, she was utterly incapable of settling the difficulties
which had been excited against her, to meet the plots which could be
formed against her authority, and to sustain the weighty charge of the
kingdom ; moreover, that she would accept as her husband, and for
the companion of her fortune and her designs, one [Bothwell] who had
the power, the will and the courage to oppose her, if she did not do
so ; and that she would never have peace with him, except by the consummation of such a wise arrangement. By these counsels this miserable man promised himself, either to reign through his confidant
[Bothwell] or to degrade the Queen, by her own act, and thus deprive
her of her authority ; all which he did. The marriage was accomplished, and the pressing solicitations of the Earl of Bothwell finally
won the heart of Mary, who espoused him in the face of the Church
with all the requisite ceremonies. Some writers have recorded that
this gentle soul was greatly persecuted by these proposals of marriage

on account of her beauty and that the facility of her natural disposition, which had not sufficient powers of resistance against the pressing importunity and the continual battle, which love arrayed against
her, brought upon her a fearful deluge of misfortunes."

Finally, to close these citations, the same author states that Mary,
even in bidding Bothwell to leave her at Carberry Hill, acknowledged
that his courage and his worth were sufficient to guarantee her against
his storm which was ready to burst upon her head. Alas! she did
not possess the moral courage to act up to the convictions of her reason.
These citations have not been made with any other view than to demonstrate that the Jesuit author, in his biography, justifies the writer
in his bad opinion of Murray, as well as in his high estimate of Bothwell, as one of the most powerful of the Scottish nobility, renowned for
the greatest exploits, of an admitted capacity sufficient to rule the kingdom, desperately in love with Mary and culpable only, or rather weak,
in suffering himself to be made the instrument of Murray and the latter's co-conspirators simply to aid him to win the woman that he
loved and to enable them to accomplish their designs. Had he been as
base and crafty as Murray, he might by a similar course of fraud, injustice and embezzlement have built up a party ; but being, in spite of
all his faults, a fearless honest man, he fell, because being alone and
without a political party he could not maintain himself against an or-
ganized party—like that which has ruled and robbed this city of New
York for so many years, backed by a fanaticized multitude, greedy
for spoil and offices.

In the following historical drama there is not an incident or remark
for which one or more authorities cannot be produced, except at the
close of the Second Act, when Bothwell is represented as coming on to
the rescue of the Queen. It is a slight anachronism. He did attempt
to rescue her at the moment, and he did so afterward, and enabled
her to re-establish her authority ; but it was not until a few days had
elapsed. Again, the language placed in the mouths of the speakers is
not, word for word, the same that they wrote or spoke ; but the ideas
are identically the same, and very often the utterances are textually
correct, with the exception that the broad Scotch or rude English of
the sixteenth century and the French is presented in the words and

forms of the present day. In all other respects, this is an attempt to arrange the momentous occurrences of the most important phases of the reign of Queen Mary in a succession of Acts, Scenes and Tableaux, so that they may be placed upon the stage with ample opportunity for a display of acting and setting such as are rarely afforded by a drama that realizes the exact truths of history and biography, without distorting or exaggerating either of them ; literally presenting, to use the words of a quaint poet—

> "The loves and troubles of Queen Mary,
> Revealed for him that reads,
> And whether she was over chary
> In all her acts and deeds."

CHARACTERS.

DARNLEY, King-Consort, Second Husband of Mary, Queen of Scotland.
JAMES HEPBURN, FOURTH EARL OF BOTHWELL, afterwards third Husband of the Queen, died in the Danish State-prison, Dragsholm.

James Hepburn, Fourth Earl of Bothwell; Duke of Orkney, &c., &e.; Third Husband
of Mary Stuart, Queen of Scotland;
as he appeared in Tournament and on the Battlefield.

THE EARL OF MURRAY, illegitimate Half-Brother of the Queen, afterward Regent of Scotland, murdered.
JAMES DOUGLAS, FOURTH EARL OF MORTON, subsequently Regent of Scotland. Beheaded under James VI., son of Mary and Darnley.
GEORGE, EARL OF HUNTLEY, brother-in-law of Bothwell.
LORD ROBERT STUART, Commendator of Holyrood Abbey, illegitimate brother of the Queen.

LORD RUTHVEN, died of consequences of fever—the relapse on his leaving his sick bed to assist in the murder of Rizzio. James VI., Son of Mary and Darnley, rooted out the family.

LORD LINDESAY, one of the most truculent of the Scottish aristocracy.

ALEXANDER, FIFTH LORD HOME, died in the dungeon to which Morton consigned him.

SIR ARCHIBALD DOUGLAS, "that priest-bred manager of plots," cousin and agent of Morton.

SIR JAMES BALFOUR "' the most corrupt man of a most evil age," betrayed by his wife, Morton's mistress, thrown into a dungeon in Morton's castle of Dalkeith.

SIR WILLIAM MAITLAND OF LETHINGTON, the Chameleon, one of the ablest and most unprincipled statesmen of his century. Poisoned himself to escape the disgrace of an infamous public execution.

SIR WILLIAM KIRKALDY OF GRANGE, an admirable soldier and experienced military leader, but a weak man, a most untrustworthy subject, and a spy, and paid agent of the English ministry. Hanged like a dog by Morton.

now enemies of the Queen, afterwards her last supporters in arms in Scotland.

SIR ANDREW KERR, of Faudonside, whose brutality at the murder of Rizzio, MARY would never pardon.

SIR GEORGE DOUGLAS, Postulate of Aberborthwick, natural son of the Earl of Angus.

SIR JAMES MELVIL, Page, then Courtier, Adviser and Friend of Queen Mary.

PATRICK BELLENDEN, a Conspirator.

THE PREBENDARY, ROBERT BALFOUR.

DAVID RIZZIO, originally an Italian Musician, Confidential Foreign Secretary or Minister of the Queen.

BETON, LAIRD OF CREICH, one of the Queen's Masters of her Household.

ARTHUR ERSKINE, the Queen's Equerry.

ANTHONY STANDEN, a gallant young English refugee, the Queen's Page.

NICHOLAS HUBERT, known as "French Paris."

HAY, LAIRD OF TALLA.

JOHN HEPBURN, of Bolton.

THE "BLACK" ORMISTON.

CAPTAIN BLACKADDER.

Retainers of Bothwell, executed under the Regent Murray.

WILLIAM TAYLOR, Darnley's Page or Body-servant.

MARY STUART, QUEEN OF SCOTS.

JANE, COUNTESS OF ARGYLE, illegitimate sister of the Queen.

MARY BEATOUN, faithful life-long favorite and attendant of the Queen. one of the "Four Maries;" niece of Cardinal Beatoun, assassinated by Kirkaldy of Grange and others.

LADY RERES, Chamber Lady to the Queen and Confidant of Bothwell.

Attendants on the Queen and Nobles, People attached to the Queen's Household, Royal Hackbutters (Musketeers), Constables for the Service of the Artillery (Artillerists), Troopers, Pikemen, &c., &c.

Bothwell—with Hagbutteers (Musketeers), Archers and Border Pikemen.

In an historical drama which inevitably requires the concurrence of so many characters, the number of actors brought upon the stage must conform to the probable strength of a company at the disposal of a single manager. Therefore, it may be necessary to reduce the number of parts, and consolidate the action and language of several persons into one representative on the stage. Thus, while the incidents of the drama are strictly true, all the characters who played their parts on the real stage of life need not appear upon the mimic boards of the theatre.

James Hepburn,
Fourth Earl of Bothwell.

AN HISTORICAL DRAMA.

ACT I.

SCENE I.—*A bosket or bower of evergreens, clipped yew, in the garden of Holyrood Palace.* MARY BEATOUN *and* LADY RERES *come forward as the curtain rises.*

Holyrood Palace.

MARY BEATOUN (*evidently continuing a confidential conversation*).
 You do amaze me, Lady Reres. Yet,
 Standing so high in confidence of both—
 Our lovely Queen and Scotland's proudest Earl—
 You must know much escapes less favor'd mortals.
 Does the Queen love the Earl, and as you say,
 With fonder, firmer force than she loved Darnley?
 Does she love Bothwell so?

LADY RERES.   Indeed she does :
And she hath found in him a nobler mate
Than any yet on whom she's fix'd her choice :
The rest were boys. In him she's found a man :
A rough one it is true, but still a man :
A diamond not all polish'd, but a man :
Hepburn's a jewel meet for Mary Stuart,
They greet at him, but such as he can scorn
The calculating, hypocritic guile
Of foxy Morton ; Knox's fav'rite Murray,
Who leaves to baser instruments the deed,
And looks at evil through, between, his fingers :
Ready to pluck the fruit when 'tis matur'd
Upon the muck heap fully fed its growth ;
And if *for him* cares not how 't grew or grows.
James Hepburn, with his mail'd and stalwart hand
Plucks the ripe ear at once with fearless front ;
He is no coward. 'Mid false, sordid " Bonds "
That rule this Scotland, he *alone* is true.
Poor he has been, despite his lofty birth.
So poor he's lack'd a single golden piece
To pay his score : yet never took a bribe
To wrong his country for a foreign quean :—
He never sold his honor to Queen Bess,
As other nobles flout at faithfulness
So that their jerkins gleam at Tudor cost.
His creed he's clung to spite of ev'ry wile,
Nor ever made, like Murray, creed the cloak
To hide intent, and set the kiln on fire
That burn'd our land, ay, to the very bone,
So that it prov'd alembic whence t' extract
Gain, influence, power, for selfish ends.
Hepburn's no hypocrite ! He loves Mary
For Mary Stuart's sake, and will not yield
A single inch to foreign lure or price,
Content to risk the loss of all he seeks
Rather than sacrifice the faith is his.
Sin ! he may sin against his own brave soul,
But never 'gainst what he deems great and true
To foster his ambition. The people
Know well that in his soul there burns the fire
For Scotland's Independence flaming high.
The nobles love him not. He scorns their lies,

Their moral weakness and their selfish strength.
However brave in brawl and shedding blood.
Among the nobles, Hepburn's not a friend ;
But 'mid the people, duly weigh'd 's the man :
There's not a lord is held in such content
And honest admiration. This makes Mary,
Despising such a coward thing as Darnley,
Seek to break loose from brilliant toy she once,
With love begotten through the eye, not reason.
So madly wed, and long to link her fate
With one who, once beside her on the throne.
Fit mate would be for queen to mate withal :
And brave as she, throw banner to the winds,
And say to England, Come what storm come may,
I and my husband will confront it boldly !
MARY B.   Each word you utter 's like revealing dawn,
Breaking through clouds after a starless night.
LADY R.   Many a village maid, in face and form—
The child of Nature 's far more beautiful
Than Mary, Queen, so peerless in men's eyes ;—
But she's a queen, therefore a deity,
And, to defects, all, blinded by her rank.
Behold in her, Anadyomene :
She's not so lovely as report declares—
Although most lovable as all admit—
She is too tall, too vig'rous in her port :
A full man's heart is beating in her bosom :
And more than once she pray'd to be a man
With helm on head and girt with sword and dagg.
Astride a gallant steed like Border Chief :
Yet in her eye there's such demoniac light
Can kindle passion in a breast of ice,
And lure, as serpent fascinates a bird : —
We've seen her do it.   Blazing into flame
Her heat could melt a lump of iron ore :
'Tis not her beauty won her Hepburn's love
But something kin to tropic heat at pole.
Magnificently clad, her lusty form
Captures the men as springtime 'livens flies :
And though she plays, as cat plays with a mouse,
With lovers bowing 'fore her sov'reign grace.
By never yielding has Earl Bothwell won :
As spell more potent overcomes the less :

And binds the weaker with more potent sway :
His magic's been an over-mast'ring will.
Her father's grandeur and her Guise finesse
Make her omnipotent in swaying men.
When young she rul'd them with her gentle lures :
A full grown woman with her subtle wiles :
And thus, pre-eminent in female guile,
She leads the wolves as Orpheus moved the trees : —
Carried away by Darnley's courtly airs.
She soon discerned the caitiff 'neath the style,
And then returning to a stifled love,
She found herself compell'd, as 't were by Fate,
To the embrace of stalwart Bothwell's arms,
As hunted deer rush wildly in the net.

MARY B.   You astonish me ! I'll keep *this* secret.
And, silent, watch th' unfolding of events :
The Queen has grown to brook no contradiction.
And visits with disfavor all who cross her—
Moreover, I remember Chastellar,
And handsome John of Gordon. I will not
Have gallant Hepburn's blood upon my conscience.
Mary is Queen. 'Tis she is highest judge.
Come let us in ! (*Church bell rings.*) I hear the Compline bell.
And as the Mass grows less in favor, we
Of the true faith must be the more attent
Upon our duties, and so please the Queen.
                        (*They go out conversing.*)

SCENE II.—*A Reve-supper in an apartment of the lodgings of the*
EARL OF MORTON, *in Edinburgh. The* EARL OF MORTON, LORDS
RUTHVEN, HOME *and* LINDESAY, MAITLAND OF LETHINGTON, SIRS
GEORGE *and* ARCHIBALD DOUGLAS. SIR JAMES BALFOUR, *and*
KIRKALDY OF GRANGE *seated around a large table in consultation.*

MORTON.   Well met, good friends : I think our course seems clear.
In our chill climate, fruits take long to ripen, but still they do ripen, even
if the sun shines out rarely. The sun has hitherto been clouded for
our projects, but it appears to me, that at last, it has burst forth bright
and warm. The Scottish masses are waking from the glamour that our
lovely sovereign cast upon them Her **marriage** with the **Popish**

Darnley sits ill on their Reformed stomachs, especially as it has been brought about by that hypocritic papal emissary, David Rizzio. To use the words of godly Master Knox, his stench is most unsavory in the nostrils of a nation, that has shown such hatred to the most dangerous enemy of our purified doctrine. Our own plan of action now must lie clear before us. In spite of the Queen's sudden passion for the bonnie long laddie, she has raised so high, even beside her in the highest seat, she now stoops to the base-born Italian lowness—

LINDESAY (*interrupting*). She covers him with wealth and dignities, and for the truckling low-born foreigner, robs us, the titled of the land. Every time I have to doff my bonnet to him—and we all must do it—it is hard to keep my dagger from her bosom. He usurps—

SIR GEORGE DOUGLAS. Do you remember, gentlemen, associates and friends, how when the nuptial ring was placed on the Queen's finger, the outlandish minion could not restrain his exultation, but in the very chapel shouted out, in monkish Latin, "Glory to God! It is done and cannot now be broken." How my blood boiled !

RUTHVEN. The Macedonian did not wait to untie the Gordian knot, but cut it with his sword, and the world still applauds the Greek's sagacity. There are swords as keen as his in Scotland, and daggers too, and men who know how to use both.

DOUGLAS. This case needs no gallant *Coup de Jarnac*, but rather the sly stick that Joab gave to Amasa, with "Art thou in health, my brother ?" (*Laughs.*) It should be done to the Italian *a la Italiano !*

LETHINGTON. We have the trail, we need but follow it. Darnley's a dolt, and, what is more, the greater dolt, in that he's drunk with pride at his uplifting. And yet he is so common in his wantonness, and finds that women yield so quickly to his Royal suit, he deems all women of the same complexion. Could we arouse his jealousy ? Remember Robert Bruce ; and the Red Comyn, stabbed at the very altar.

KIRKALDY. Lethington, have you no thought of God, nor fear of Hell, to counsel thus !

LETH. Heaven ! Hell !—Bogles to frighten children. My Laird of Grange, although you are a man of blood, a soldier, "a stout man, who always offers, by single combats and at the point of the sword, to maintain whatever you say ;" and I a penman rather, I have as little a fear of what men dread the most as any belted earl or swordsman ever buckled on a breast-piece. Heaven and Hell are stories framed by priests and preachers to frighten children, not to scare grown men. Your conscience and your pride of orthodoxy will be your ruin. Pride must have a fall ! I can read you without glasses. Your squeamishness will at some future time get you with all your conscience into a terrible scrape.   You are not so cold, my Laird of Grange, that the warmth of Mary's glances has not already stricken home, clean through your polished cuirass.

KIRK. (*starting up, and laying his hand on his sword*).   My Lord of Maitland !

MORT.   Quarrelling, my lords, before the hunt's a foot !   Give me money, women and authority, and I will not quarrel with the means by which I get them !

LETH. (*perfectly cool and without moving*).   My Laird of Grange, your very heat betrays you.   You are very like the good people of Laodicea, neither cold nor hot enough—Look to it!   Lukewarm drinks set ill upon the stomach, and lukewarm people ever come to grief.

MORT.   Peace ! peace ! my lords, we are forgetting Scotland and the holy cause we represent.

LETH. (*aside*).   Hypocrites one and all ; but I must pull each set of wires, so that my various puppets dance at the proper time to the piping I deem the fittest for the occasion and my purposes.

MORT.   What are you muttering, Maitland ?

LETH.   Simply, Kirkaldy should be grateful, not irate.   I but warn him !   Has he forgotten Chastellar and Gordon ?   They loved Mary, and what came of it ?   The hangman's noose ; the axe!   My Laird of Grange, if Mary Stuart ever makes you love her, beware lest Cupid's knot turn into a halter to choke even you, the pink of chivalry.

KIRK. (*rises indignantly*).   Maitland ! do you dare to insinuate that I, Kirkaldy, am another maker (minstrel) or traitor. (MORTON *interposes*.)

MORT.   Lords, this is no time for discord.   Our country—well, not to feign, our interest—needs us, and we need ourselves in fittest mood for counsel and for action. (MORTON *crosses to* KIRKALDY, *and pacifies him*. LINDSAY *addresses* LETHINGTON, *in dumb-show, deprecating further irritation*.) Lethington speak !   You are the coldest heart and subtlest head among us ; what is your plan ?   My Laird of Grange, be patient !

KIRK.   Patient !   Ay, patient !   My Laird of Maitland, you are— so says the general voice—a Roman philosopher, a stoic.   Look to it yourself, lest you so entangle yourself in your own ,net you cannot extricate yourself with all your cunning ways.   Although you may not fall upon your sword like the stoic-soldier, Cato, you may yet take a drink like Demosthenes, the Athenians' greatest orator, to save you from a worse than halter.

LETH.   Well spoken, Laird of Grange.   Now you have said your say and had your quip, and have shown your knowledge of the Humanities ; now hearken to my plan.   Mary, our gracious Queen, is but a woman after all, and brought up in a court where she learned more than prayers.   She came to us heralded by stories of anything but fair

Lucretia's self control, and these have followed her. The holiest of our brethren still believe that Chastellar's head was cut off to keep his tongue from telling tales of how she lured him on and played with him and worse. This present favorite, Rizzio, is so high in her good graces that he is with her at all hours, day and night. Make Darnley once believe the Italian's had *his* rights and he will join us to make way with Davie. This will rouse the Queen—her Guisan blood. She is already disgusted, wearied with this boy-husband ; his humors and his mistresses. Davie sent whither (*points upwards and then downwards*), who knows whither—Darnley must be disposed of. Mary then must have a lover bold, handsome, high in rank ; one who, to possess the woman and to wed the queen, will stop at nothing and will venture everything. We must so manage it, that the new man will rid us of this Darnley ; but, in the doing of the deed, so outrage public opinion that when Mary, carried away by passion, gives her hand to him, all Scotland will rise up like one man to drive him out and punish both.

MORT. A second Ahithophel !

DOUG. It is to be hoped that no Hushai will be found to traverse so goodly a plot.

KIRK. This seems like seething a kid in its mother's milk. And what of Murray ? What will he say ? Will he take part in this?

LETH. Yea and nay, not openly ; but he will look at it approvingly betwix't his fingers.

(*All laugh again, and good humor is restored; all rise, consult together, and then, after exchanging opinions, resume their seats.*)

KIRK. But, my lords, this is all well enough for talk ; but where will we find the man who will play our game, and yet be so chivalric in his disposition, so void of guile, so manly, and, even more and better for our projects, so filled with love of Mary, he will not see into the secrets of our Bond ?

SERGEANT (*without below, at the entrance door of the dwelling*). Guard, turn out ; stand to your arms! Ain High and Mighty Lord, the Earl of Bothwell ! (*All rise and look at each other, as if seeking to divine each others thoughts.*)

LETH. (*smiling aside*). My leaven works !

USHER (*without, at the door of the apartment, and preparing to throw it open*). Ain High and Mighty Lord, the Earl of Bothwell !

(*All turn toward the door.*)

LETH. (*in a low tone, significantly*). Where is our man, my Lords ? (*In a low voice.*) There is the very man ! (*Pointing to the unclosing door.*) Here, now ! (*The valves of the door are thrown wide open.*) Welcome ! You come in time, my Lord of Bothwell !

(*All rise and greet BOTHWELL with effusion, who becomes the central figure of the Tableau as the Curtain falls.*)

Holyrood Palace.

ACT II.

SCENE I.—DARNLEY'S *apartment in Holyrood Palace, beneath the famous room known to history as the Queen's Bedchamber. This scene should be so arranged that, when it opens (or rises), it will allow full space for a reproduction of* MARY'S *Bedchamber and Cabinet or "Closet," in the rear of it, so that the latter (Scene II.) will be shown when Scene I. draws aside or opens, is drawn up or sinks.*

DARNLEY (*pacing nervously to and fro, stops every now and then as if expecting some one. His hands play with his dagger which, at intervals, he spasmodically, half-unsheathes and thrusts back again violently into its scabbard*). King and not king, husband and yet not head! She plays with me! Am I not her husband? Twice married, doubly in possession : handfasted, tried, accepted, married, crowned : and yet, what power have I? Murray is driven forth it is true, but he is ever present in his friends : cold, cruel Morton : sly, calculating Lethington, and all the rest, who have the people's ears; ay, and though John Knox possess the people's hearts. I am but a puppet, a toy, a cicisbeo, not as good! Then there's that wild fearless mosstrooper, stick-at-nothing Bothwell. I know not where he stands, I cannot comprehend it. Sometimes I think the Queen loves him, has loved him always, ever since he and I sought her in France, at Joinville, fifteen years ago. But let that pass. We will look to him hereafter. Rizzio 's the present man; the knave, the sneaking cunning dog I trusted. The Virgin curse him! I 'll have his blood before the midnight strikes; his heart's blood! He 'll never thrust himself after to-night, between the Queen and me. Do I love

her ? I hate her now ! Did I ever love her, or was it Scotland's
crown and throne I coveted ? Ha ! Here is my chief reliance.

(*The clank of armor is heard without, and* RUTHVEN *enters. He
wears a long loose gown, but under that, is clad in full panoply as if
about to take the field, except as to his helmet, which he carries in his
hand. A nightcap instead muffles his livid brow. He is deadly pale and
walks with difficulty.*)

DARN. My Laird of Ruthven, you startle me: you look like a very
bogle.

RUTHVEN. And nearly am one. Have I not arisen from a sore bed of
sickness, to help in an act of justice due to my King and kingdom ?

DARN. Justice ! Yes, it is justice to put away the thing that stands
between the King, nobility and husband, and owns both Queen and
wife, the kingdom—all, all, all ! Ever since that night I found the minion in the Queen's bed-chamber, and the door barred between my wife
and me, my blood has been boiling with fever's heat and force. This
night ends all. Be you all ready ? I will have open the door and keep
the Queen in talk till you come in. Remember, be alert, for only one
man at a time is able to mount the narrow stairs. This night, shall
it not end all, my lord ?

RUTH. Assuredly, if your own courage is as hot and lasting as you
say your fever-fit has been. But come, our friends await us, and the
hour has struck on every bell that notes the time in Auld Reekie.

Exeunt.

SCENE II.—*The scene opens and discovers the famous cabinet within the bedchamber of Queen* MARY *in Holyrood Palace, so well
known through pictures, descriptions* and photographs. The position of the characters should be arranged in exact accordance
with the historical pictures.* QUEEN MARY *and* JANE, COUNTESS
OF ARGYLE, *are at supper.* RIZZIO *is likewise seated near the table ;
his lute resting against his chair, as if he had been singing. The
Queen sits in a double chair, of which one seat has been left unoccu-
pied for* DARNLEY. BETON, ERSKINE *and* STANDEN *in attendance.*

MARY. Minstrel, resume your song : although it is not as joyous as
becomes the theme.

---

* "The apartments (of Holyrood House) occupied (1822) by the Duke of Hamilton,
fill the old portion of the Palace. On the second floor are those [once] occupied by
Queen Mary, whose bed still remains. The furniture of this bed is of crimson damask,
bordered with green silk tassels and fringes, and tradition assigns the decorations to

Rizzio (*takes up his lute and sings to the accompaniment of this instrument*).

> You ask me what is love ?　Oh, sweet !
> 'Tis clothes, 'tis fire, 'tis drink, 'tis meat ;
> 'Tis anguish, rapture, life—'tis wings ;
> Of earthly happiness the springs !
> A crowd confus'd of hopes and fears,
> Of smiles and ecstacy and tears ;
> Of heaven on earth it gives the taste :
> And without love this orb 's a waste,
> Chaotic sphere like chilly moon :
> A jangling rhythm without tune :
> Then grant me love or take me hence,
> For without love this life 's offence.

---

the fair hands of the unfortunate queen ; but the whole is now in a very decayed state. There are likewise some old chairs, covered with crimson velvet ; in this room a small opening is to be seen, which leads to a trap-stair ["a piece of wainscot, about a yard square, hangs upon hinges, opens on this trap-stair."—Brewers' "*Various Palaces.*"] communicating with the apartment below. By this passage Darnley and his accomplices conveyed themselves into the closet in which Mary was supping with her secretary, who was dragged out of the Closet through the Bedchamber into the Chamber-of-Presence, and there expired under repeated (56) blows."—"*Views in Edinburgh.*" 1822.

"Queen Mary's Bedroom.—A chamber twenty-two feet one inch, by eighteen feet six inches ; the ceiling divided into panelled compartments of diamond and hexagonal form, adorned with the emblems and initials of Scottish sovereigns ; and the walls are hung with tapestry, illustrative of the mythological tale of the Fall of Phæton. ⁂　　⁂　　⁂　　Here stands, with fragments of the blankets, the bed of Queen Mary, the decayed hangings of which are of crimson damask, with green silk fringes and tassels, and the chairs and table, &c., are of the same period. The Queen's work-box is on the table at the bottom of the bed. The needlework represents Jacob's dream, and is said to have been worked by her own fair hands. The Baby-basket of James VI. is on the stand beyond the bed; it was presented to Queen Mary by Queen Elizabeth on the birth of the Prince. *The door opposite on the right, half hidden by the tapestry, leads to the secret staircase by which* Darnley *and his infamous associates ascended to the royal apartments to assassinate* Rizzio. *The one on the left leads to the little apartment so famous in Scottish Story* as the scene of the assault upon the unfortunate Italian, in the presence of the Queen. Every one whose imagination is at all vivid, will here easily realize the particulars of that terrible event;—the Queen forcibly restrained by Darnley—the overthrown table and scattered viands—the fierce and scowling conspirators pressing into the little room—and the dagger left sticking in the body of Rizzio. who crouches behind Mary for protection. From this closet the assassins dragged their victim through the other royal apartments, stabbing him as they went, until he fell dead at their feet at the top of the staircase, by the door of the audience chamber. To this room the brutal Ruthven, reeking from the slaughter, returned and demanded a cup of wine; and here probably it was that the conspirators threatened to cut the Queen " into collops " if she dared address the populace from the window."

Then grant me love or take me hence.
For without love this life's offence !

(*He gazes a moment on* MARY, *as if awaiting a responsive look, and receiving none, puts down his lute with a sigh and lapses into a revery.*)

MARY.   Ah, Messire David, you are in a sad mood to-night.   (*Takes the lute, tunes it, and sings to a rattling accompaniment*):

Love,* whence comes it and whither goes ?
Love, how increaseth, chills to close ;
Love, what is it ?   No one knows.

Love, who can explain it, its raptures and woes :
Love, true love, e'er stronger, e'er lovlier grows.
With the grace of the lily, and perfume of rose.
'Till hearts it has blended take long last repose.

Love, true love, 'tis body and soul,
And spirit combined in one exquisite whole,
And playing together, when perfect, one role.

There, that is music I like.   But, hark !   What do I hear ?

BOTHWELL (*without and below*).

SERENADE.

Queen, soul, love, mine !
My first thoughts at waking, my last thoughts on sleeping.
When slumber is creeping, resistance o'er leaping.
Are thine and all thine.

Like moon in calm beauty, my vows all salute thee ;
Thy beams on my slumbers, in rapture transmute me—
Ideas divine !

Like sun in his splendor, I waking adore thee :
Thy glories recalling, I prostrate implore thee
Be mine, ever mine !

All radiant with graces, thy inner lights lend thee.
In beauty perennial may blessings attend thee !
Be happiness thine !

---

* " L'Amour est, je ne scais quoi ;
Qui vient de je ne scais ou ;
Qui finit je ne scais comment ;
L'Amour vraie finit toujours en plus."

Thy slave and thy lover, in constancy ever,
Let nothing the ties which unite us e're sever :
May the ivy yet twine

Their fetters for both of us, loving and waiting :
Hope daily for both with new happiness freighting,
Till at last thou 'rt mine !

For that I live dreaming, so eagerly dreaming—
The future, though distant, yet ever sure seeming,
For thee still I pine !

DARNLEY (*enters from the private stair leading from his apartment, be-*
low, into the Queen's (his wife's) bedroom. MARY *turns toward him with*
affectionate greeting. He sits beside her in the double chair. They kiss
each other and embrace; he steals his arm about her waist and clasps
her to him, as if they were on the best of terms.)

MARY. My lord. have you supped ? Shall I command another course
for you ? I thought you must have finished your supper by this time.

DARNLEY (*evasively*). I need no supper. Do not let me interrupt your
meal. (*As he speaks the tapestry concealing the Secret Passage into the*
Queen's Bedroom is raised and RUTHVEN *shows himself*).

MARY (*startled by the clash of his armor and ghastly appearance of*
RUTHVEN, *whispers to* DARNLEY). What does this mean ? Why
comes this bold bad man; my mother's foe, my own ? I thought he
was dying. I meant to visit him, for although he is a murderer and a
villain, he is the husband of my aunt. What means his naked sword ?
Is he distraught ? Has he escaped his watchers and comes to me for
safety, deeming himself pursued by the avenging ghost of his murdered victim, Charteris ?

RUTHVEN (*who has seated himself while she has been whispering to*
DARNLEY). I come here for your good.

MARY. Good ? Do you look or act like one who comes for good ?

RUTH. (*pointing at* RIZZIO). Yes, madam, for your good ; to rid you
of that minion. There is no harm intended to your grace, nor to any
one, but to yonder poltroon, David.

MARY. What has he done ?

RUTH. Ask the King, your husband.

MARY (*to* DARNLEY, *who has risen and is leaning on the back of her*
chair). What means this ?

DARN. (*faltering*). I know nothing of the matter.

MARY (*pointing to* RUTHVEN). Then away with him.

(THE LAIRD OF CREICH, ERSKINE, STANDEN *and attendants advance*
upon RUTHVEN *to put him out ; but he keeps them off with his sword.*) ·

RUTH. (*defending himself*). Lay no hands on me! I will not be handled.

(*As he is speaking the cabinet is invaded by Conspirators, who advance upon* RIZZIO *with menacing miens and threatening gestures. The* QUEEN *interposes herself in defence of* RIZZIO, *who draws his dagger which, manifestly, he has not the courage to use, and, falling on his knees, grasps the hem of her robe and hides his face in its folds.*)

MARY. What is the meaning of this? Do you seek my life?

RUTH. (*making a pass with his sword at* RIZZIO). No, madam; but we will have out yonder villain, Davie. (Mary *seizes* RUTHVEN *by the wrist.*)

RIZZIO. Guistizia! Guistizia!

MARY. If my secretary, Signor Rizzio, has done anything amiss, the Lords of Parliament shall try him; but the usual forms of justice shall be observed.

ANDREW KERR OF FAUDONSIDE. Here are the means of justice. (*Produces a rope with his left hand and with his right presents a dagg or pistol, which he presses against the bosom of the Queen, who confronts him intrepidly.*)

RIZ. (*speaking with great terror*). I am a dead man.

MARY. Fear not, Signor Rizzio! The King will never suffer you to be slain in my presence; neither can he forget your faithful services. (DARNLEY *is abashed and about withdrawing.*)

RUTH. Sir, take the Queen, your wife and sovereign, to you. Pin her arms! Remove her!

(*Clamor without.* A Douglas! a Douglas! *Conspirators rush upon* RIZZIO; *the table and chairs are overset, the* COUNTESS OF ARGYLE *seizes a candelabra as it is thrown down and saves the robes of the Queen from being enveloped in flames. For a moment all is dark: then followers of* MORTON *rush in with torches. A dreadful struggle ensues, all the conspirators striving to stab* RIZZIO, *who grovels at the Queen's feet, she still endeavoring to shield him.* RUTHVEN *seizes the Queen and throws her into the arms of* DARNLEY.)

RUTH. (*to the Queen*). Do not be frightened; there is no harm intended you. All that is done is your husband's deed.

(MARY *struggles to free herself while in the arms of* DARNLEY.)

RIZZIO, *grovelling at her feet and clinging to her dress, is crying, stammering and repeating,* Misericordia! Guistizia! Mercy! Madam, save my life! Guistizia!

MARY (*to* DARNLEY). Out upon you, dastard! You did come to betray me with a Judas kiss. You will live to remember this—your Judas kiss. (*To the Conspirators.*) Traitors and villains! Begone! or you shall suffer the law's severest penalties. I will protect this hap-

less creature, this innocent victim, this faithful servant, even although
to him I owe this bitter moment, because that he won from my unwill-
ingness a consent to wed the caitiff wretch now dares restrain his
sovereign.

RUTH. This has lasted too long. Have out that gallant ! (*indicating*
RIZZIO).

DARN. Let him go, madam ! They will not harm him !

RIZ. (*shrieking*). Save my life, madam ! Save my life, for God's
dear sake.

GEORGE DOUGLAS (*snatching* DARNLEY'S *dagger from its sheath, and
stabbing* RIZZIO *over the Queen's shoulder, leaving the dagger sticking
in the wound*). This is the blow of the King !

KER. (*pressing his pistol against the Queen*). I will shoot you dead
if you any longer struggle to save your minion.

MARY. Fire ! If you do not respect the royal infant in my bosom.

DARNLEY (*pushes away* KERR'S *dagg or pistol, which misses fire, as*
PATRICK BELLENDEN *makes a stab at the* QUEEN *with his rapier. The
blow is parried with a torch by* ANTHONY STANDEN, *her page.* DARN-
LEY *forces the* QUEEN *down into a chair and holds her there while* RIZ-
ZIO *is torn away by the conspirators, and amid terrible uproar and
oaths, clash of weapons and attempts to slay him*).

RIZ. (*as he is hurried out*). Guistizia ! guistizia !

(*Renewed and terrible uproar and cries without, then groans and
cries of exultation, followed by a thumping sound as of a body thrown
down stairs. The Conspirators gradually struggle back into the room,
laughing and jesting with each other, wiping the blood from their
weapons, and readjusting their garments.*)

RUTHVEN (*throwing himself, insolently, into a chair*). Give me a
drink. Bring me a cup of wine ; I am sore felled by my sickness.

MARY. Where is Messire David ? Whither have they dragged
him ? Has he been put in ward, and where ?

BEATOUN (*sadly*). Madam, it is useless to speak of David, as the man
is dead.

MARY (*to* BEATOUN, *sorrowfully*). Dead ? Ah, poor David, my good
and faithful servant ! May the Lord have mercy on your soul ! (*To*
DARNLEY, *savagely.*) That was a Judas kiss.

(*A pause, grouping and tableau.* MARY *suddenly springs up and
rushes to the window and throws it open, and shrieks for assistance.
Through it is heard the clamor of an aroused populace and the clash of
arms, and through the casement streams in the glare of torches carried
by those without. Behind the scenes noise of fighting.*)

MARY. Help, help, my lieges ! (DARNLEY *drags her away from the
window.*)

RUTH. Madam, if you make such an outcry, sooner than these people should rive you from us, I would cut you into collops, and throw them down to the rabble.

MARY. Where can I look for aid?

(*Noise of fighting without, and cries:* Viva Bothwell! St. Bride for Bothwell! Spears and axes! Bothwell! Bothwell!

MARY (*falling into a chair*). Always faithful to his motto, "Kiip trest!" My own brave Bothwell! I will trust him.

(*Through the main entrance to the chamber burst in the* EARLS OF BOTHWELL *and* HUNTLEY *with a body of serving and kitchen-men armed with spits, cleavers, knives and whatever weapons they could seize or came to hand. Their sudden inburst drives back the Conspirators and frees the* QUEEN. BOTHWELL *rushes to the* QUEEN, *who throws herself into his arms.*)

MARY (*to* DARNLEY). Ah! traitor and son of a traitor! Is this the recompense you give me, who have loaded you with benefits, and raised you to dignities so great and undeserved? Is this the reward you reserved for him who did so much for your good and honor? (*Wiping her streaming eyes.*) Ah! no more tears, but revenge! No more joy for me until your heart shall be as desolate as mine this night. I will now study revenge! (*Half swooning.*)

RUTH. (*sinking, overcome with faintness, into a chair*). A thousand devils! What have we here? Furies and hell! Curses on Maitland's policy and plan! We have slain the jackall here and let the lion go. Besotted fools, our work is all to do over again!

(*Behind the scenes.*) Long live the Earl of Bothwell!

(*The Conspirators prepare to renew the struggle,* BOTHWELL *confronting them triumphantly with the* QUEEN *in his arms.* DARNLEY *abashed contemplates the group, not knowing what to do. As the fighting is about to be renewed, the Curtain falls.*)

Edinburgh Castle.

ACT III.

SCENE I.—*Same as Act I., Scene I.* MARY *and* BOTHWELL *come forward from the arbor in amorous discourse.*

MARY. Darling, the history of my loves is but a serial story of mishaps. Love, the sum total of a woman's life, has realized for me the verses of the Latin poet, that "love's a spring of delights, and afterward a season of despair." Dearest, you well know that I am versed in the Humanities, and most conversant with those poets, troubadours and versifiers of the affairs of the heart. Love, they say, is a mingling of honey and of acid, a "bitter-sweet." Mine has been indeed a bitter-sweet in which the former, bitterness, was the most potent. Yet no one will forego the sweetness of the entrance thereunto, even if the judgment doth assure the bitterness of the exit. It is indeed a most tempting bait that entices the poor fish to gorge its own destruction. My own Bothwell, young in years and in experience, I did love the boy Francis; but I had not then known you. I did lament him, but I had not as yet felt the first effects of the intense influence that your manliness, fidelity and mind exerted on my soul of souls. This varnished toy, this Darnley, and you came to me in my first months of sorrow. To whom did my heart cleave? To you! To whom did it incline at Joinville and at Jedburgh? To you, to you, to you!

BOTHWELL. And yet you allowed that traitor bastard, Murray, to drive me into exile.

MARY. Alas, my love, I am unpardonable, but (*bewitchingly in tone and manner*) I was powerless. That man, that betrayer, my father's son, was all powerful; and, weak as women always are when they should be strongest, I yielded. I am without excuse. State policy—

my curse upon the sad necessity—compelled the sovereign where the woman should have been all queen.

BOTH. I forgive that because I went, and the event proved all that I could wish. You were compelled to recall me. But you married Darnley.

MARY. The peace and stability of Scotland compelled me. The Queen of England drove me to the act. I was the tool of her accursed policy, the property of her ambition. You were in exile : woe is me that I consented to do so ! I was without a friend to aid me. France, Spain, England, Rome, were providing me with husbands; Murray was depriving me of everything but the name of Queen. How, but by marriage, could I put a stop to the persecution on the one side, or have crushed the insolence of the other. Oh, my dear love, well you know that it was not then in my power to make choice of you, unless I would have been content, not only to have my crown torn from me, but also to resign both our lives to glut the implacable malice of our foes. I never loved this Darnley, and his ingratitude has made me hate him. Oh, my Bothwell, you must condone my wedding elsewhere than as my heart desired. I believe that in your heart, your wise and manly heart, you must now be perfectly convinced that there was an invincible necessity for this hated, hateful marriage, although the fury which filled your soul to behold me in another's arms would not permit you to acknowledge it. And yet, my own, my own dear Bothwell, my own dear life, I was, I am, I ever shall be yours and only yours.

BOTH. My own Mary, if this was and is so, where was that trust, you ever do protest, in me, when you, in spite of Darnley, made me your Lieutenant-General and, afterward, Warden of all Three Marches, an office never before held by one person :—ay, placed your Hepburn, omnipotent upon the Borders, as a barrier against England; and nathless, was afraid to call him to your aid against so many nearer but less dangerous enemies, you fear and feared.

MARY (*caressingly*). Not with you thus, here, by my side.

BOTH. Love of my youth, my manhood, and my prime; my truest life, my own Mary; you confess all this, and yet you gave yourself to him; this upstart, senseless, graceless, long-legged boy—more like a woman than a man : merely a lusty, beardless lady-faced Adonis; such as your astute uncle, the Cardinal of Lorraine wisely styled him, "a high-born quarrelsome coxcomb;" totally unmeet to be my own Mary's consort.

MARY. Think not, my Hepburn, it was love that furnished me with arguments to justify my choice of this ingrate caitiff, for I protest by that dread power, by which I have so often sworn, that Bothwell was

the dearest thing on earth ; that he is so, and ever will be so while I
have life.

BOTH. (*with a touch of sarcasm*). You bore with him full long, and
it me seems that Hepburn and his loyalty were clean forgotten.

MARY. I married Darnley through policy's compulsion, not from
choice. Surely the fire of true love never enkindled my affection for
him. No time is pleasing to me that is not spent in giving you new
demonstrations of my affection for you. Well may I err in the rules of
government and state, when all my thoughts are taken up with love
for you. If I had to choose whether to relinquish crown and state, or
thee, my Bothwell, I would leave my dignity and kingdom to follow thee
throughout the world, a simple damsel. I never deceived you and
remit myself altogether to your will. Send me at any time advisement
of what I shall do, and whatsoever may come of it, I will obey you.

BOTH. And say you so ? The time is come to prove it. Were you
once free to love, not as now and in the past, in secret, but before the
world, to wed, to crown, where would you be ?

(*As he utters these words and gesticulates, he spreads abroad his arms,
questioning, and* MARY *throws herself into them.*)

MARY. Where would I be ! Where my heart has been for many,
so many years, my Bothwell ! Here ! here ! here !

BOTH. Then you do trust me now ?

MARY. Implicitly, my hero ; my knight, my MAN ! Do you think
your Mary can ever forget the accomplished knight and fearless horseman who, at the Tournament near the Rood of Greenside, galloped in
full panoply down the steep side of the Calton and leaped his steed into
the ring, to the terror and admiration, not only of his Queen, but of her
whole Court ? You seemed that day the god of war, in grace, incarnate !

BOTH. Then let us in. (*Pointing to the arbor in the background.*)
The sun is near his setting. Night, which brings counsel as a rule ;
this night will bring release and usurp the privilege of day. All is
prepared as planned with your consent, assistance, wishes and commands. There let us rest awhile in fond commune and with your kisses
seal firm the bond hereafter makes us one—forever one.

(*He uncloses his embrace after kissing her passsionately, and then,
with his arms thrown about her neck and hers twined around his waist,
they disappear in the arbor, whispering fondly as they go.*)

BOTH. (*within the bosket, sings*) :

Mary, my Queen !
When banished from thy presence dear,
The world seems desolate and leer,
And steeped in gloom :

My actions spectral movements seem,
I do not live, but idly dream ;
   The world 's a tomb,
Till, at thy coming, light and life,
With beauty, grace, and glory rife,
   My thoughts illume.

What, then, to me is Scotland's ban ?
My soul dilates, once more a man,
   The world I dare ;
For thee I live, for thee would die—
Yea, for one glance of thy fond eye,
   And nothing care ;
Beside thee smiling, all is light ;
Absent from thee, the world is night,
   Mary, my Queen !

                    (*Scene changes, or opens.*)

SCENE II.—*Interior of the notorious building in Edinburgh, known as the Kirk-o-Field.* Time, night of 9th–10th February, 1567.*

   As the space between the stage and the arch over it is very lofty, and the actual rooms represented had very low ceilings, there must be a double flooring, showing DARNLEY'S *sleeping apartment over Queen Mary's room, in the latter of which the powder (with which the building was blown up) was stored, under* DARNLEY'S *bedchamber.*

   Upper Stage (U. S.) signifies DARNLEY'S *bedchamber. Lower Stage (L. S.)* QUEEN MARY'S *room.*

   In the apartment (U. S.) DARNLEY *is discovered reading, in company with his body-servant or page,* TAYLOR.

   QUEEN MARY, BOTHWELL, *the Conspirators,* cum suis, *first show themselves on the stage below and afterward mount a staircase to the Left Side facing the audience. The commencement of this staircase might be shown laterally, so that the course of their ascent would be recognized by the audience and nevertheless leave the whole of the upper portion of the upper stage clear for the action of the piece.*

   L. S. *Enter* MARY *with her train, and the Conspirators, Nobles with Attendants, lighting them with flambeaux or torches, and* BOTHWELL *following. He is richly but soberly attired.*

---

   * KIRK-O-FIELD.—The house of Kirk-o-Field, as Buchanan, the literary organ of the conspirators, declared, "was the most unwholesome, horrible and dangerous place to which an invalid could be brought."   *   *   *   It was not. "The contrary has

BOTHWELL (*approaching* MARY *to the front, leaving the rest in the background*). The passion kindled in my bosom sixteen years, since when first we met at Joinville, in the sunny land of France, when my "White queen" was widow, the widow of a boy, who, with all his fondness, could never fill the soul of one fit for a Cæsar's mate. For sixteen years this passion has fed upon my heart, nourished by hope and faith. My love was like the morning sun, obscured by mists and clouds ; it was felt, not seen. But when at my lone headquarters at the Hermitage, you deigned to visit your poor wounded knight, it seemed as if the mists and clouds all fled. Then followed your sojourn at Glasgow. Your letters by French Paris assured me I had won the game on which I had staked my life. And now the sun has attained meridian height. Will it shine out and in splendor ? This night the blow will be struck which shall decide whether that sun shall stand still in full noontide blaze, as it stood still at Joshua's command on Gibeon, or sink in storm and ruin. Thou hast said and writ, that thou art all my own. When the crack comes which sends hence this unruly boy, wilt thou stand to it. The only obstacle is thus removed and if thy purpose holds, then, then thou art mine, before the world, as thou hast

---

since been demonstrated by the Medical Faculty of Edinburgh uniting in choosing it for the site of the Royal Infirmary ; in fact, the ground is at present occupied by the College. The Thief's Row   *   *   *   was neither more nor less than the Sanctuary of our Lady's Kirk-o-Field, which remained, like that attached to the Abbey of Holyrood, long after the dissolution of its monastic foundation. Whatever might be said of the badness of such a neighborhood, applied no less to the Edinburgh Palace of the Regent Hamilton, where his brother, the Primate of Scotland, was then residing within sight and hearing of everything going on in the lodgings chosen for Darnley. The Mansion itself was a substantially built edifice only two stories high, with a basement or cellar which served for the kitchen and offices.

A spiral staircase in a turret, defended by what was then called, and is still called in Scotland, a turnpike, on the same plan as a wicket turnstile, communicated with the private entrance through a low postern-door in the Town-Wall, and gave access to both chambers through their respective lobbies. Behind these were the small apartments called *garderobes*, in which the attendants slept ; and considering the fact that no less than five perished with Darnley, and that one absented himself that night, and another was taken out alive, they must have been strangely crowded.

Scotch dormitories were, however, arranged for persons of inferior rank very much in the manner of berths in a steam-packet, in recesses in the walls, masked with sliding panels, of which many examples may still be seen in ancient castles, as well as the Highlands hotels and cottages."   STRICKLAND's "*Mary Stuart*," I. 386.

See "Murray's Handbook for Scotland," 58 (2) : "Kirk of Field lay almost due east by south of Edinburgh Castle, about half a mile : and a little more than that west by south of Holyrood Palace. Drummond street, leading out of South Bridge opposite the College, occupies in part the site of *The Kirk-o-Field*, in which stood the house occupied by Darnley, which was blown up, *with him in it*, as was generally but erroneously supposed. 9th—10th February, 1567."

long been mine in secret, and as I have been wholly thine since the first hour we met.

MARY (*looking round upon her suite and finding that they are absorbed in conversation, and not observing her*). All that I wrote from Glasgow and spoke, even this very evening in the palace garden, I felt and feel. There 's not a thought I placed on paper and sent thee by French Paris, but that I felt and feel. Take thou the hand that held the pen and try my pulse! Does it beat calmly?

BOTH. (*after taking her hand and holding it a minute*). Like clockwork. Like the tides obedient to the laws that never change; strong, full and regular.

MARY. So holds my purpose. Is everything prepared?

BOTH. Even beyond our hopes. These Lairds with whom I hold this Bond are neither true to thee nor me; but faithful to themselves; yea, they are fiercely true to their own common interests, as is the love that fills our souls for each other. Darnley this night must die! Even though the whole powder-plot should fail, he dies as surely as if an earthquake were to heave and split the soil, and swallow up these walls and all within them. There is not an enemy he ever made but circles it in arms; and the few servitors that feed and fill the mine are nothing to the numbers who compass Kirk-o-Field without. Fear nothing! If all the powder I have brought from Dunbar should but suffice to lift the roof, there is enough of it stored beneath the very walls' foundations to send them soaring.

MARY. How? You amaze me!

BOTH. This Bond, distrusting Bothwell's courage, has made their vengeance "sicker," and plotting with me have plotted against thee and me and Darnley, that their vengeance fail not. Not only he and his, but the very stones of Kirk-o-Field will kiss the stars to-night if there 's virtue in saltpetre.

MARY. My own, my own true knight; my Bothwell! But, hark! Our conversation has lasted long enough. We understand each other. I leave early, soon, thou knowest, to grace Sebastian's wedding at the palace. A few short sweetened words to lull this man's distrust and I will forth. Then see thou to it! Be wary! Let no suspicion light on thee—nor me; but— FAIL NOT!

Queen MARY, *and her suite, likewise, and* BOTHWELL *leave* (L. S.), *ascend the stairs, and enter* DARNLEY's *chamber* (U. S.). *The Attendants with torches exeunt, withdrawing to one side.*

The action (U. S.) *for the most part, is in dumb show : the Nobles paying their court to* DARNLEY; MARY, *apparently, conversing affectionately with him.*

L. S. *As soon as* MARY *and the others are thus occupied* U. S., *enter*

from the rear, through the postern, BOTHWELL'S *followers,* HUBERT OR-
MISTON *and* HAY OF TALLA, *bearing sacks of powder.* HUBERT *or*
FRENCH PARIS *lighting them with a candle.*

U. S. BOTHWELL *suddenly leaves* U. S. *and descends by the stairs to* L. S.

BOTH. (*to his followers*). My heavens, what a din ye make! They
may hear above all ye do. And how you look, Hubert! all be-smirched
with powder! Heard ye not what the Queen said when she saw
you? "Mercy, Paris, how begrimed you are." Wash your face and
hands and look innocent, if you have pluck enough. (*In a low tone
communing with himself.*) Most curious coincidence! Like the pale
horse of the fourth seal in Revelations: the White Steed of Death
transported hither from Dunbar, the fatal sacks will send Lord Darnley
up—or down—which way he goes it matters not, so that he goes.

(*The attendants signify obedience to* BOTHWELL'S *warning and having concealed the powder with tapestry and the hangiugs of the bed,
go out* (L. S.) *through the postern.* BOTHWELL *re-ascends to* DARNLEY'S
apartment U. S.

U. S. DARNLEY (*Evidently pleading with the Queen*). My queen!
my wife! desert me not! Let us once more be one, as erst we were;
one table, one bed, one life. Grant this, oh! sovereign lady, or your
poor Henry doth not desire ever to leave this room a healthy man
again. Oh! be once more my loving bride of Weymiss and of Stirling,
and I will go wherever you do list. Let us be as in our better days,
before I sinned, together at bed and board, and live like wife and husband!

(FRENCH PARIS *shows himself, unseen by* DARNLEY, *at entrance door*
(U. S.), *signalling that all is ready.* MARY *makes a sign, that she understands.*)

MARY (*kissing* DARNLEY, *and placing a ring on his finger; with a
smile*). Sweet, you are an invalid! You are nervous! You are fearful!
There is no recipe against fear. It is time you were abed (*distant bells
toll eleven*). Eleven is striking. It is later than I thought. I must not
break my promise to Bastian and his bride. My lords and gentlemen,
see that the torches are lighted. I will return on foot.

(BOTHWELL *and the Queen's suite quit the apartment* U. S., *descend
the stairs and leave the house* L. S. *Through the open door by which
they go out flashes in the glare of the flambeaux or torches, as they
are lighted.*)

U. S. MARY (*throwing her arms around* DARNLEY'S *neck*). Good
night, sweet! We will see more of each other hereafter. (*Kisses him,
then, aside.*) Kiss for kiss. You kissed me as the signal for poor Davie's murder; I kiss you as the signal of my revenge and my emanci-
pation. Kiss for kiss!

DARN. (*with his arms around her waist, strives to detain her ; she unclasps his hands and gently places him in his chair, and throwing kisses at him as she goes, draws near the door at the head of the stairs,* U. S., *stops, and then with a changed demeanor, and with emphasis, addresses* DARNLEY.

MARY (*significantly*). This time last year, and about this hour—poor David Rizzio was murdered. (*With the last words she passes through the door* U. S., *and descends to* L. S. TAYLOR *lighting her down the stairs. She goes out through the main entrance, left side,* TAYLOR *closes and locks the door,* L. S., *after her ; then goes into the Queen's bedroom, and tries the postern* (L. S. *rear.) Assured that it is locked, he passes out of the door opening upon the entry, locks it* (L. S.), *ascends the stairs to* U. S. *and rejoins* DARNLEY, U. S., *who has started up from his chair as the Queen spoke her last words and continued, while* TAYLOR *is absent, gazing at the door as if absorbed in reflection upon what the Queen had said.*)

DARN. (*to* TAYLOR, *as he enters*). Heard you what her Majesty said on leaving.

TAYLOR. I did my Lord. The words were ominous. It is just eleven months to-night since Signor Rizzio was slain.

DARN. Those words were like a black bull's severed head, portending sudden, violent death or murder, here in Scotland. They seemed to drip blood on my ears, as they fell from her lips, even as she kissed me. My soul is sad within me! Oh! I remember! I remember! Mine was a Judas kiss, that night. Such was her declaration after the plot revealed itself in blood, and Rizzio was dead. (*Wringing his hands. A Judas kiss—then—that it was. Oh! I repent me! Was her kiss to-night another Judas kiss ? Woe is me! Why do I recall this, at this moment ? (Prays silently.*)

TAY. Take courage, my good lord; the Queen may not have intended anything. Her words may have been an accidental freak of memory.

DARN. (*not attending to* TAYLOR's *attempt at comfort*). What did she mean ? What could she have meant ? And, yet, she was so kind. (*Looking at the ring* MARY *had given him.*) And gave me this, and promised to return and give me more of her good company henceforth—and yet those words. They sounded like a menace. It likes me not. (*Seating himself.*) Draw the table hither, and trim the lamp! Bring the Breviary, and read the Fifty-fifth Psalm. I cannot sleep. Those words have banished sleep.

TAY. (*obeys, brings a book,* DARNLEY *settles himself into an attitude of listening and* TAYLOR *proceeds to read in a low voice, inaudible to the audience. Dumb show.*)

L. S. *While this action is going on* U. S., *the postern* (L. S.) *is unlocked, and* FRENCH PARIS *enters with a smaller bag of powder, unties it, and lays a train from the bed to near the door, and finally adjusts to it a piece of lunt, (slow-match). Simultaneously* BOTHWELL *appears at the door, with a slouched hat drawn over his face and draped in a trooper's cloak, watching the proceedings. Behind him, looking over his shoulder, stand* HEPBURN, ORMISTON *and* HAY OF TALLA. FRENCH PARIS *lights the slow-match, goes out of postern hurriedly, closes and locks the door. The slow-match flickers, sputters, but does not burn.*

U. S. DARNLEY (*starting up suddenly*). Heard you no noise below ?

TAY. (*after listening*). None, my dear Lord.

DARN. I am so nervous, so unmanned, so weak from sickness and faint-heartedness. I must go forth into the garden to breathe one breath of the fresh air.

TAY. You will catch your death of cold, my Lord !

DARN. (*forcing* TAYLOR *aside, who tries in vain to detain him*). I'd rather die a thousand deaths of cold without, than freeze to death with terror here within. (*He thrusts* TAYLOR *aside violently, catches up a furred cloak, and followed by* TAYLOR *rushes through the door* (U. S. *left*), *springs down the stairs, opens the main entrance door, left side, and flies out.*

As they disappear (L. S., *rear*).

BOTH. (*without*). I have watched the match through the key-hole It does not burn. Unlock the door ! Let me go in and see to it.

(*Sound of struggling without.*)

FRENCH PARIS (*without*). Oh, go not in, my Lord ! Oh, go not in ! Tempt not your fate, my Lord ! You will perish ! Have patience, my dear Lord ; for the Queen's sake, have patience ! If not for your own sake, for the Queen's sake forbear !

All is now quiet without and within—a pause of a few minutes— suddenly the slow-match flares up ; kindles the train ; the fire runs across the room ; the powder explodes ; the house blows up and falls in ruins, and through the shattered rear (representing the outer wall of the house) are seen the corpses of DARNLEY *and* TAYLOR, *strangled, lying dead on a sort of terrace, so as to be distinctly visible from the front. View of Edinburgh and Arthur's Seat in the distance. Immediate clangor of bells and cries of the alarmed neighborhood. Amid the uproar the voice of* SIR ARCHIBALD DOUGLAS, *at the extreme rear, is distinctly heard.*

BALFOUR. Eternal good night to my Lord Darnley ! The deed is done, and well done !

As the smoke drifts away, the din without increases ; other bells ringing alarm, join in amid the deafening clangor. Curtain falls.

Bothwell Castle.

ACT IV.

SCENE I.—*An Apartment of the Suite occupied by the* EARL OF MUR-
RAY, *in Edinburgh. Date, 8th April,* 1567.

The curtain rises upon MURRAY, *in earnest discourse with* MOR-
TON *and* LETHINGTON, *discussing the affairs of Scotland.*

MURRAY. It grieves me sorely to find myself all powerless to avert
such evils from my country ; to see my sister falling completely in the
snares of such a man as Hepburn, the profligate, the simple sworder
and however brave—no man can deny his valiantness—so utterly de-
void of principles we follow as our guides.

MORTON. Murray, between us, who understand each other thoroughly, what need is there of empty words. It is with us as with the old
Roman augurs; they could scarcely look each other in the face without laughing. Such utterances as yours, my lord, are giff-gaff. Your
goal is supreme power. You thirst, you hunger, languish for the
crown, or at least the sovereign authority denied by birth, by accident.
You talk too much and are too squeamish. You do not object to eat
the cosset when the butcher has dressed it for your table; but shrink
yourself from killing it or even standing by to see the butcher slay and
flay it. You talk too much. When we had kept your skirts all clean
and clear of Rizzio's taking off, so that the poor thing, your sister,

verily believed you innocent of blame, and claimed your sympathy, and gave you her confidence, you needs must talk and over-act the part. Again, when Darnley was blown up and opportunely, and your noble countess was taken sick and summoned you to her side, you needs must talk anew, and the whole country rung with words you dropped in going to her. What was repeated showed you were all privy to the plot. Away to France. We made short work with Rizzio and with but little space got rid of Darnley. Set off for France! Leave all to Lethington and me! This man, this Bothwell, has not risen so high, but that we can fly a hawk will bring him down. He is too honest. He thinks he can rule without a party. No man ever could do that ; rule by sheer force of will, of loyalty. He dreams that devotion to his country, to Scotland, "Land o' the Leal," and his still stronger passion for the Queen, are all that is needed.

Mur. Bad as they say we are, I must admit (*laughing slyly*) that among our *blackguards* Bothwell is that *rara avis,* a *white* crow, a miracle of virtue.

Mor. Make no delay, blindfold the Queen ! Never was woman so ductile in the hands of anyone can play on her affections ; so easily cajoled. Consign your only child, your daughter, to her wardship, and remit to her best offices your countess ! This will be a blind. This very trust will allay all her suspicions.

Mur. But, meanwhile, you take no count of Bothwell. Maitland, my Lord of Morton, seems too sanguine.

Lethington. Bothwell's sun is soaring to its noon. Never a sun arose that did not have a setting, some sooner and some later. The days are short in Scotland, except in summer, and summer's not yet come. As yet 'tis early spring, with weather most uncertain. The coming summer must be all ours with its long days and longer twilights. Before the summer solstice, Bothwell's day will have been swallowed up by night. The game is ours. We hold the winning cards. (*Significantly*) I hold the ace of trumps ?

Mur. (*eagerly*). The ace of trumps ? How ? Who ?

Leth. Kirkaldy, Laird of Grange.

Mur. Kirkaldy ?

Leth. Ay ; you seem astonished. You do not note the setting of the wind as does an eye, like mine, that is ever fixed upon the vane of popular opinion and circumstances. Kirkaldy is a mere soldier ; a good one, it is true, but nothing more. His head is not well balanced, and his heart impressionable. Already he casts sheep's-eyes upon your sister, and she returns his gaze with sympathetic glances. Poor woman, I would pity her did she not stand between us and our fortunes ; but pity is too precious a commodity to throw away. I admit that she loves Bothwell with all the passionate ardor of her double nature. She comes by it honestly. She has it from her father, the late king, who gave so many noble sprouts to Scotland; and from a mother, the woman of Lorraine, the Guise. And, more, report assigns to her prime favorite, the gay gallant, gracious Cardinal Bentoun, the authorship of Mary Stuart. Mary herself, although so dead in love with Bothwell, that she denied long since no proofs of it; long, long before we recognized the fact; yes, loved him back into the days when she wore weeds for Francis—nathless, she had an eye meanwhile for others; Damville, Chastelard, John Gordon; nay she went so far as to handfast and then wed Darnley; loving this Bothwell all the time. She is a born coquette; not bad, but easily twisted around a subtle finger. Leave all to us, to me! Kirkaldy is my ace of trumps! As Morton says, "Away to London, to Elizabeth, to France: be patient: bide the time!"

James Stuart, Earl of Moray.

MUR. (*who has listened attentively and reflectively, and marked the drift of all these arguments*). My mails are all prepared. Keep me advised! My amplest influence and most puissant backing you have —may use them to the uttermost: but save appearances. Keep me clear from blame, and, if I grasp the sceptre, rest assured we will divide. Farewell. (*Exit.*)

LETH. (*as* MURRAY *goes out*). God speed ! (*To* MORTON, *who has latterly remained somewhat in the background ; silent, but intent on every word that passes*). Divide ! Yes, that we will, or your proud day, my Earl of Murray, will be as short as Darnley's was, as Bothwell's shall be. (*Extending his hand to* MORTON, *who grasps and shakes it assentingly.*) Now, for Kirkaldy ! to plume the popinjay, and set him up, so that his vivid colors shall attract our bird's attention.* Then, with dulcet piping on our part, all safely hid, we'll tole her into the trap we have set. After that, when Mary's taken, *away* with the popinjay ; into the dust heap with him ! I must follow Murray, to get him off for London and to France ; our work brooks no delay. (*Exit.*)

---

* Here the question suggests itself, Why did Mary permit herself to be deluded by Kirkaldy ? Was she, like many women of her class, suddenly overcome by a wild spasm of passion for him—one of those outbreaks which Bothwell so greatly feared after his marriage with her, and against which he guarded her and his honor with the ultra suspicious jealousy of a Spaniard ; or did she believe, as the celebrated English historian Lord Mahon, expresses it, " No one, perhaps, except the immovable Knox, was able to bear up against them [her charms?] Her transcendant beauty [?] was joined to the most bewitching manners, and few even of her bitterest enemies could help doing homage to the mastery which she thus exerted over the hearts of men."

" But her mental gifts were still more remarkable. Acuteness, grasp, readiness, and fertility of resource were all characteristic of her intellect. The subtlest statesman could not circumvent her. The most practised reasoners failed to get the better of her in discussion. Menace could not daunt, danger rather inspirited her. We have said that Knox' was invulnerable to the graces of her person and the witchery of her manners ; but it is plain, even from his own reports of interviews which took place between them, that he was no match for her in argument. The greatest of English queens was her contemporary, and in some respects her rival, but even Elizabeth's genius looks pale when confronted with the brilliancy of Mary's. *She seemed indeed born to rule the world, and had her self-control been at all proportionate to her courage, her talent, and her beauty*, she would in all probability have accomplished results in her day that must have had an enduring influence upon the destinies of Europe. BUT THE STRENGTH OF HER PASSIONS RUINED ALL. ☞ *Combined with her penetrating intellect and her noble physique, there was an emotional nature as ardent as it was unscrupulous.* ☜

" It is when we take all these elements into consideration, and view her conduct in the light of them, that alone we have any chance of dispelling the almost enigmatic obscurity which has appeared so long to surround her history."

" At the bar of impartial justice, Mary Stuart stands convicted of having been 'Act and Part ' in the murder of her husband, Darnley.

" As to the other point of her having acted under the influence of *a guilty attachment* to Bothwell, *there is still less room for hesitation.* Let any one only read over that Apology for her marriage, which she transmitted to the Guises of France, and it must be obvious how painfully she flounders between truth and falsehood. Everything, indeed, points to the same conclusion. That most unseemly visit of hers to Bothwell, at his Castle of Hermitage ; that mockery of justice by which he was acquitted of having any share in the murder of Darnley ; that ABSURD STORY of the Queen's ravishment, which it is impossible for any candid reader to peruse without seeing that, like Horace's girl, the Queen was but *male pertinax* in the matter ; those passionate expressions which she uttered of her determination to cling to Bothwell, even after it was clear that to do so would prove her ruin, all lead to the same conclusion—that

Mor. (*looking after him with a subdued cunning laugh*). Am I alone of iron ; as Murray often saith, impenetrable ? Am I the only Lord in Scotland that is proof against this Mary Stuart ? And yet, it seems to be so. Little does Maitland dream that I see through him as through all the rest. Away, Earl Murray ! Justly, Maitland looks beyond, and thinks that as he rolls each stone up, slowly or swiftly, but ever surely, to the edge of the beetling crag, that he can topple over each in turn and, then, at last, Mary remains queen, with Maitland, her Prime Minister. He

James Douglas, Fourth Earl of Morton.

counts without his host. Morton will hold over. Morton, who knows no love nor lure but interest. When Kirkaldy has served Murray's turn

she was laboring under *an almost insane passion* for the worthless profligate." (Why use such terms of the "great Earl " ? Was he worse than his peers ? No ! Was he as bad ? No ! Was he far better ? Yes. He was honest, loyal and intrepid.

It is quite needless to call in, for the decision of this question, the famous Casket Letters. These may or may not be genuine. *We have no doubt ourselves as to the verdict which should be returned regarding them.* But our purpose is already accomplished without their aid. *The guilt of Mary, is to our mind clear as any proposition in Euclid,* and the *bona fides* of Buchanan is vindicated. That there may not be errors, extravagances and exaggerations in his "*Detectio,*" we do not maintain. These are in-

and Lethington his own, as he supposes, in truth mine, he too must go and Morton reign as Regent nominally ; in fact, with England's backing, as dictator, King in all but name, supreme.   (*Scene changes.*)

(*A lapse of eleven days* is supposed to occur between this Scene and Scene* II.)

————— ♦ ———

SCENE II.—*The interior of the famous "Annesley Tavern" in Edinburgh, after the termination of the historic "Ainslie Supper." Time, after midnight,* 19th–20th *April,* 1567. *Visible evidences, to the rear of the stage, that a grand banquet is just concluded. The wax candles in the candelabra have guttered away or burnt down. A long disordered table is strewn with the relics of a feast ; goblets and flagons upset upon the table, around which appear many chairs and stools, some still upon their legs and others overturned. Several of the guests, overcome with wine, are being helped or carried out by attendants, others are being cloaked. Cries are heard without summoning the horses and suites of noted guests.* BOTHWELL, HUNTLEY, MORTON, LETHINGTON *and others stand apart, talking over what has occurred.*

BOTHWELL *and* HUNTLEY *disengage themselves from the groups and come forward ; the rest go out by the rear door.*

BOTHWELL. You must admit, my brother, that never was a ticklish piece of business better managed. With all my hopes and strong abiding faith, I scarcely could have counted on such an unanimity. Why all signed willingly, except that sneaking Eglinton, who stole away so quietly, he disappeared like a very wraith. Here I hold the Bond (*showing a roll of parchment*) signed by at least five bishops, the bastard, Murray, nine earls and seven lords of little less account, among the high nobility, papists and protestants alike, counselling and urging the Queen to marry me. It sets forth that she cannot find throughout the world a nobler or more fitting mate, endowed

———

cident to all men who write as near as he did to the date at which the events recorded actually took place. But his substantial accuracy is established, and however much our romantic or sentimental feelings may be wounded, *we must, in deference to historical fact, admit that the beautiful* QUEEN MARY *was, in reality,* ONE OF THE MOST ABANDONED AND UNSCRUPULOUS OF HER SEX."

* In order to indicate the intervals, the longer or more important lapses of time between the Scenes in Acts IV. and V., it might be advisable to drop an inter-act curtain, as Irving does, at the end of Act II. of his adaptation of "The Merchant of Venice," after the elopement of Jessica and Lorenzo, and lift it again to exhibit the return of Shylock to his desolate home.

with all the qualities most proper for the station. By it they pledge their lives, their fortunes, and their honors to sustain and maintain the marriage and its consequence, *fas et nefas:* nay, what is more and stronger, therein they invoke upon their souls the stigma of being accounted unworthy and faithless traitors, neither worthy of reputation nor credit at any time thereafter, if they violate their pledges as signed by them (*pointing to the signatures on the Bond or roll he holds*). Never in Scotland was there signed a stronger Bond, or one of which the intention was more clearly manifest. Is it not so ?

HUNTLEY. Assuredly, you have the adhesion of the major part of the most powerful peers and strongest hands and intellects in Scotland.

BOTH. (*unrolling the parchment and pointing to the leading signature*). And, see, my old enemy, James Stuart, leads the roll. It is true he was not present, but that is in keeping with his cautious character. I hardly thought he would sign, but his second self, his Machiavel, that arch devil, Morton, or the Chameleon, Lethington, cajoled or coaxed him into it. However, I ought not to be so much surprised after all, recalling that after Darnley was sent so opportunely to his appropriate place—even before I was acquitted of all art and part in the grim work : and while the miserable rabble of the capital and so many of the better classes of the burghers were wildest in their underhand as well as open accusations against the Queen and myself—he had the courage to give me a grand banquet in his lodgings, to testify his full belief in his royal sister's innocence and in my own, of any participation in the death of that unfledged booby and bustard with fine legs.

HUNT. Ay, and thereby to the world gave best assurance that he, at all events, was certain that you, my dear Bothwell, was entirely free from guilt.

BOTH. (*with a quiet laugh*). Considering that in intention and in everything, save that his hands were neither black with powder nor red with blood, the 'bastard' was as guilty as any one of us. I had a right at least to thus much countenance and backing. He is a sneaking dog, who aye makes his fangs meet in the leg behind when the wolf is close beset in front; but never flies at the throat, unless the rest of the pack have crippled the quarry. Huntley, you must confess, and you have reason to do so, that he is a dangerous—if but a sneaking tyke.

HUNT. Much as you have occasion to hate Murray for the past, how much more I ; my race's ruin, my father's death, my brother's judicial murder ; all, all were due to him. To you I owe my rehabilitation ; my life can scarcely pay the debt. (*Extending his hand, which* BOTHWELL *grasps with fervor.*) In life and death I am yours ; command me.

Both. Brother, I am right glad that of your own accord and without any solicitation you speak so strongly. Can I count on you ?

Hunt. (*raising his right hand, as if affirming what he says*). I repeat, command me ! Simply express your wishes, and what you wish is as good as done.

Both. (*again exhibiting the roll of parchment that he holds*). You see this Bond ! It recommends me as the most proper husband for the Queen ; although I am a married man and my wife is your sister. I must be divorced. The Queen desires, Scotland needs the sacrifice. It is a hard condition, but let your sister Jane consent and I will endow her richly for the future. The Barony of Haddington and all its ample revenues shall be assigned to her and hers forever. As for you, the House of Gordon shall be most richly recompensed and lift its noble head as rich in land and appanage as in its palmiest days.

Hunt. (*after a thoughtful pause, then sadly but firmly.*) These *are* hard lines, James Hepburn ; but I consent. Your marriage with the Queen has now become an absolute necessity for her, for you, for Scotland : ay, for me, and necessity knows no law. Again, I repeat (*giving his hand to* Bothwell), for life, for death, command me ! Now, what more ?

Both. Delay is our worst enemy. Nowadays things move fast and every hour lost is pregnant with peril and augmenting difficulties. The next step is to publicly gain possession of the Queen's person. This must be done through the semblance of a ravishment. She has consented ; she is all ready to hoodwink the good people. I must carry her off to my grim Castle of Dunbar. After she has been there, alone with me, you understand me, Huntley, for some half a score of days or so, and in my power absolute, with her consent, connivance and full will, she must wed me (*significantly*) to save what little reputation she has left. In fact the thing stands so there is no time to lose, even to save what little credit has been left her by Murray, Morton, Maitland and their crew.

Hunt. (*starting*). What do you mean ?

Both. The answer must be spoken *in* your ear, so that no second ear can catch it. (*He whispers a few words to* Huntley, *who by gestures expresses the greatest astonishment.*)

Hunt. (*with bated breath, stammering.*) What ! What ? By you ?

Both. (*lays his fingers on his lips*). You now understand that any delay is impossible.

Hunt. (*shaking his head*). No, no ; indeed no !

Both. Now off with you, you most astonished man. Make all your preparations and your moves in strict accordance with the plans that I here give you. (*Takes two folded papers from the bosom of his doublet, and hands them to* HUNTLEY.) The smallest is for you. Deliver the second, largest, to the Queen. After she reads it, let me have due answer as fast as horse and man can bring it. Keep me advised from time to time. I have ever lived up to the fullest meaning of the motto of my house, " Kiip trest !" Be faithful ! I will be ready ! See that you get a good ready likewise ! Now, good-night. After all this, are you with me ?

HUNT. Again I repeat, command me ! I am yours for life, for death. (*As he speaks these words, he half draws his sword from its scabbard and thrusts it in with an audible snap, as if to accentuate his words.*) For life, for death ! Good-night.

BOTH. Good-night, my brother ! God be with you ! Good-night !

HUNTLEY *goes out by the main door in the rear ;* BOTHWELL *stands lost in thought for a moment, then brings his hands together with a loud clap, as if perfectly satisfied, and leaves the room by a side door.*

The scene (*III.*) *closes in front of the banquet table and disorder in the rear, so as to allow ample time to clear the stage, behind, during the succeeding Scene III.*

Between Scenes II. and III. about four days are supposed to elapse. The other intervals between the following scenes can be intimated by the dropping of an interlude curtain.

SCENE III.—*At the Fountain- or Almond-Bridge (Foulbriggis) between one and two miles outside the old walls of Edinburgh, and about three-quarters of a mile distant from the Castle on the Old Linlithgow road, which entered the capital by the West Port. Time, High-noon, 24th April,* 1567.

BOTHWELL (*enters from the right hand, followed by Captain* BLACKADDER, *both are in full armor. To those without*). Halt ! Captain Blackadder send out patrols and make such dispositions, that no party from the West, many or few, upon the causeway, proper, on a by-road or across the fields, can reach the West Port without being intercepted. If a company should present itself in arms and make a show of fight, attack them instantly, but shoot no shot nor arrow. Do the work without noise and with cold steel. See to it ; I trust to your experience and discretion. (*Exit* BLACKADDER L. H. *Drawing off his gauntlet and extricating a letter, which he reads.*) This is from my ladye-love. She tells me that until she lay at Linlithgow last night she had an escort of three hundred horsemen, but, there, got rid of them. My

sweetheart is no fool and twists men round her fingers as deftly as she threads her needle.—Moreover, she bids me bring with me, a force full strong enough to crush out any opposition. I have anticipated both her fears and wishes, and a regiment more trustworthy in every respect, never followed a leader for a desperate adventure. (*Noise of a galloping a horse without,* L. H.)

PATROL (*without*, L. H.) Halt! Dismount! Whence? Whither?

FRENCH PARIS (*without*). A friend, from Linlithgow; dispatches for my Lord, the Earl of Bothwell.

PATROL (*without*). Pass, friend; but leave your horse.

Enter FRENCH PARIS, L. H.

BOTH. (*eagerly*). Well! Have you a letter; any token?

FRENCH P. Nothing; none is needed, mighty Lord. Everything is as you ordered. The Queen is even here, and has with her not to exceed a dozen riders.

BOTH. Any men of note?

FRENCH P. The Earl of Huntley, Sir William Maitland of Lethington, and Sir James Melvil. The rest are grooms and jackmen.

(*Renewed trampling of horses, without,* L. H.)

PATROL (*without*, L. H.) Halt!

CAPTAIN BLACKADDER (*without*, L. H.) Welcome, illustrious Princess!

MARY (*without*). What means this armed array? Where is the Earl of Bothwell?

BLACKADDER (*without*). A bow-shot distant by the bridge.

MARY (*without*). I will dismount: I am weary of the saddle; Huntley, Maitland and Melville follow me. Let the valetaille bide here.

MARY *enters* (L. H.), *accompanied by the* EARL OF HUNTLEY, LETHINGTON, MELVILLE, *and Captain* BLACKADDER *in the rear. These no sooner appear on the stage than a body of dismounted jackmen (spearmen) enter from both sides and form, so as to close every exit from the stage to any one.*

As MARY *advances* BOTHWELL *rushes to meet her, and kneeling kisses her hand. Before either can speak* MELVILLE *steps suddenly forward to separate them.*

MELVILLE. What means this violence?[*] Earl of Bothwell, does this mean ravishment? This is foul treason!

BOTH. (*with a sudden burst of fury*). False meddling fool, I'll stop your interference for all time, and send you to find out if that which your coadjutor Maitland doth deny exists; to Hell!

---

[*] Melville's sudden burst of loyalty is a very slight anachronism. It occurred elsewhere, but it did take place, and Mary barely saved her life.

(BOTHWELL *jerks out his dagger and strides furiously towards*
MELVILLE. *The latter partially shelters himself behind* HUNTLEY,
while MARY *throws herself between them.*)

MARY. Spare him, my Lord! For my sake, spare him. He is not
worth your anger. He is no soldier, he is a mere courtier. He meant
no harm; he merely asked what I now ask. Why do you meet me
thus in arms and force?

BOTH. (*aside to.* MARY). Need we dissemble longer? (MARY *makes
an affirmative sign.*) Captain Blackadder, look to these gentlemen.
My Lords, Earls Huntley and Maitland; yes, Sir James, even you,
you are in no danger for yourselves, but a mighty peril threatens
her majesty in Edinburgh. This, I am here to prevent. She must
away with me to Dunbar. Within its walls she is safe from every
menace. With your permission, mighty Princess, we will set forth at
once. (*Aside to* MARY.) Can you stand the journey. You know
the road and distance well. (MARY *makes another affirmative sign, only
visible to* BOTHWELL.) Captain Blackadder, get the men to horse; but
sound no trumpet. We needs must arouse no question in the city.
Send on ahead half a dozen of our best mounted troopers in order
to have everything prepared and fitting for the reception of our sovereign lord, the Queen. Despatch! (*Exit* BLACKADDER, L. H. *An
alarm bell rings out in Edinburgh.*) Hark! there is no time to lose!
French Paris, conduct these gentlemen to their horses.

(*Exit* HUNTLEY, MELVILLE, LETHINGTON *and* FRENCH PARIS, L. H.)

BOTH. (*blows a whistle.* Enter, R. H., HAY OF TALLA). Laird of
Talla, leave a strong rear-guard to cover and conceal our movements
and keep back all pursuit. If possible, do not take life. (*A cannon
shot, without, from the Castle of Edinburgh.*) Curses upon the fool!
what means the Governor, Sir James Balfour. Can I trust that man?
What means that shooting from the Castle. My Laird of Talla, we
must not be pressed. You know your business. (*Another alarm bell
rings.*) Ha! the Tocsin of St. Giles! (*Significantly.*) If necessary,
kill! The Queen needs easy riding. We must not be pressed.

LAIRD OF TALLA. Make yourself easy; I know what you mean. I
have made all my dispositions. (*Makes a military salute and exit,* R. H.)

Enter, L. H., CAPTAIN BLACKADDER.

BLACK. The advanced guard has marched. The Laird of Talla has
some four hundred good sturdy men to hold the rear. The main body
is composed of the pick of the whole force: they are in the saddle.

BOTH. (*to the Queen*). If you are ready, let us go.

MARY (*smiling, aside*). Ready, aye ready. (*She extends her hand to*
BOTHWELL. *He takes it, kisses it and leads her forth,* L. H.)

BLACK. (*following*). I told that dry old quiz, Sir James Melville, that the Queen was ravished with her own consent. I rather think he'll find it so, and to his sorrow, when, once, he gets to Dunbar. (*Exit,* L. R.)

Between Scenes III. *and* IV., *an interval of an afternoon and evening is supposed to elapse.*

———·———

SCENE IV.—.*In apartment in the Castle of Dunbar (destroyed within three years by the* EARL OF MURRAY, *after he had become Regent). Time, the night of* 24th *April,* 1567 ; *the same day* BOTHWELL *met Queen* MARY *at Fountain or Almond-Bridge, near Edinburgh, and had escorted her to the Fortress of Dunbar, of which he was Castellan.*

Ruins of Dunbar Castle.

BOTHWELL (*now in half armor, booted to the thigh, leads in* MARY, *still equipped for riding. He enters, speaking with severity, as if to others behind the scenes*). Look to yourselves, my Lords! We brook no interference. Blackadder, restore their swords and relieve them from guard and let them go. Although they are my foes and unfriends to the Queen, they need not fear if they comport themselves in peace and offer neither counsel nor resistance to my purposes. (*To* MARY.) This ends the farce and need of it. Why was it necessary that I thy lover should be put to this, and seem to seize at Fountain-Bridge, by force, what has been mine for years, my other self, my very self, my Mary ?

MARY. 'Tis better so. This seeming justifies that upon which I have been long resolved. Although I have so often lain within thine arms—thy wife in all but the mere name—I yearned to be thy wife by right, all that I had been years, in soul, ay, a twelvemonth in very deed.

BOTH. It scarcely needed this ; but still thy wish was law to thy true knight. When at that Annesley Supper eight earls—besides that subtle traitor, thy bastard brother, Murray, who had signed before—five bishops and eleven barons subscribed the Bond, pledging themselves, their sacred honor and their powers, to defend me against every calumny and charge of wrong doing, and avowing I was fittest mate for Scotland's queen, what need then of a seeming ravishment. When the wife, you made me wed, Jane Gordon, and her brother, earl and head of her house had, for a price—the Barony of Haddington and its dependencies—bargained, consented to a divorce ; and Jane and I agreed that we should be put apart by every court has cognizance of such affairs in Scotland ; it seems, to use the language of your creed, a work of supererogation to act the part of a foul ravishing. But still, my love, you willed it, and it is done.

MARY. Oh, Bothwell, little does your fearless heart understand my painful situation. Many, oh how many, flout your love for giving up her heart to thee, although acquitted by thy peers of all complicity in the murder of the wretched Darnley.

BOTH. (*interrupting her*). Murder ! What term is this to me ? Did I not act in strict accordance with your wishes, else had I done the deed openly, in the sight of day, yea, fearlessly, as I slew Elliott of the Park or would slay any one that came between thy heart and hand, thyself and me.

MARY (*laying her hand caressingly on his arm*). Bothwell, *my* James, between *us* this is comedy ; but to the world a tragedy. Could I, by blood a Guise, be ignorant of the growing popular force and influence (*scornfully*)—out upon the hour that the people came to have a voice in the affairs of sovereigns ! They must be conciliated with a show of deference to their opinions. We need but show a little defer- ence—would I could better play the part—to blind them, lead them, rule them, as we will. This is but statescraft, policy, and conquers as surely as the slash of sword and crash of cannon. Now I am in thy power, in thy castle, helpless ; a lone woman, in the grasp of one ac- cused of conquering our sex by magic arts and philtres—nay, be not angry—fiercely as my soldier storms a breach.* Where do I now stand ?

* While so very many pens—anxious to enlist in the romantic role of knight-errants —have devoted themselves in the endeavor to clear the character of Mary, invest her with more than mortal faculties, and even ascribe to her poetic genius, great powers at versification—which she did not possess—and assign to her the attributes of a real martyr—which she was not—since a true martyr must be, not only a victim, but an in- nocent one: every such romantic pen and pencil have ranged themselves with the

What foreign prince would seek the hand of Mary after the daring
gallant, James Hepburn, had held her helpless over-night in his stronghold alone, without a chamber lady. (*Sadly.*) No sovereign prince: nay,

---

ranks of those devoted to the misrepresentation of her only true lover, her only con-
-tant and loyal champion, Bothwell. Michelet demonstrates how little truth can be
placed in Brantome's testimony against him: and invalidates that, the only contemporary evidence, as to the want of manly beauty and grace in her life-long lover and
third husband. Mary's statue in Westminster Abbey is as much a proof against her
touching transcendant physical beauty as the only existing picture—the basis of
all others—known as the Hardwick portrait.

She was not beautiful in the real sense of the word, but through other faculties as
fascinating as a Circe, and Bothwell was, according to disinterested pen-portraits, an
eminently attractive man. No authentic likeness of him exists, and—as is now almost
universally admitted—he was a man renowned for qualities the most alluring to the
opposite sex, and possessed of a loyalty beyond or equal to any proof and of a con-
summate courage, such as that with which even mythical heroes are seldom endowed.
The fact is, he would rather kill than coax.

Even Gilbert Stuart—Mary's great partisan—drew a better picture of Bothwell, and
gave him a higher character than the majority of historical writers prior to this gen-
eration ; and Hosack, the Queen's Advocate, represents him as endowed with the
noblest qualities a man can possess.

Stuart writes thus (160-2, 230-1, 237) : " The breach between the Queen and her
husband was already too great; and he [Murray] studied to make it irreparable. The
Earl of Bothwell has acquired an ascendency in her councils; and he [Murray] courted
him with assiduities and flattery. Mary herself was eager to bind them together in a
lasting amity, and fancied to add to her happiness by the firmness of their union." * *

James Hepburn, Earl of Bothwell, was born to an opulent fortune, and to an
hereditary command over numerous retainers. *His fidelity to the crown had discovered
itself during the struggles of the Reformation.* His zeal, services, and *sufferings* in
that boisterous period, were distant recommendations of him. In the Rebellion excited by the Earl of Murray, his exertions were later and more interesting. But what
chiefly *endeared* him to Mary, was the support he had afforded her against the mur-
derers of David Rizzio. It was by his means, in a great measure, that she was enabled
to recover her importance, and to chase them out of her kingdom. Her gratitude to
him was excessive ; and he improved the favorable impressions he had made, with un-
ceasing *courtesy* and attention. By her favor he rose to *exercise all the power of government.*   *   * A boundless love of power, a fearless corruption, and a riotous
prodigality were his characteristics.   *   * He could scheme the most criminal
enterprises, and was desperate enough to put them in execution.   *   * *A
polished exterior rendered his vices more dangerous.* HE WAS IN THE PRIME VIGOR OF
LIFE ; AND HIS PERSON AND BEHAVIOR WERE ATTRACTING. A passion for pleasure involved him in intrigues and gallantry. A taste for trifles, *elegance of address,* and
softness of manner, so alluring to women of every condition, heightened the complais-
ance with which they naturally survey the imperfections of the voluptuous. ("*His
merits, his address, his assiduity* and his persuasions overcame her." 230.)   *   *
To establish himself in greatness, he was ready to perpetrate whatever is most
flagitious, and could think without emotion of treachery, poison, and the dagger. The
Earl of Murray, whom he wished to employ as a ladder to advance him to grandeur,
penetrating into his character, availed himself of it ; and he was utterly overthrown by
a man, whose ambition was not less extravagant, but whose abilities, DISSIMULATION,
and refinement, were far more transcendent and profound."

not a scion of a royal line would seek me for a mate, now that I have
been thy spoil. (*Gaily.*) Nay, darling, if thy sweetheart marry must,
she'd have to courtesy humbly for the hand of one of Scotland's rude
and haughty lords—all whom I hate and loathe save thee, my love,
my long-loved, trusted and faithful Hepburn. Yes, if I took a subject
to my bed it could not be without the general feeling that what you
rapt by force, by force you had enjoyed. Now, do you see into my
little plot ? The world knows not how long I have been thine in truth :
thine every way. The game is now played out. We can afford to

"This fatal promise [to marry Bothwell], while it invigorated all his passions, gave
a relief to the painful agitations of the Queen. The recentness of her terrors disposed
her the more readily to give admittance to softer sensations ; and he had too much
gallantry not to press this advantage, and to display all the ardors of a lover. He even
affected to have fears of the disappointment of his love. All her feelings were exquisite ; and he knew how to awaken them. The elegance of their entertainment, of
which he had previously been careful, their solitude and the near prospect of their in-
dissoluble union, invited them to indulge in the delirium of pleasure. During twelve
days she was under the dominion of *a young and agreeable*, a daring, and an unprincipled profligate ; skillful in seduction and accustomed to impose on female frailty ;
*who could read in her look the emotions of her heart, and the secret workings of forbid-
den desires ;* allure her mind to give itself up to the power of the imagination and the
senses ; take a pastime even in her pangs of remorse, and make them act as a zest
to enjoyment ; mark the conflicts and the progress of expiring virtue ; and exult in
the triumphs of sensibility over shame."

"After that Bothwell had anticipated with the Queen the tenderest rights of a husband, it was proper to think of the ceremonial of their marriage."

"It was only by slow degrees, and by habits of caution, vigilance, and address,
that he could hope to be formidable. With the assistance of the Queen, it was his first
care to uphold the splendor of the court ; and, *immediately after the marriage, the
Board of Privy Council reflected a heavy lustre to him by its distinction.* There assisted
in it, the Earls of Huntley and Crawford, the Lords Fleming, Herries and Boyd, with
the Archbishop of St. Andrews, and the Bishops of Galloway and Ross."

Crawford tell us Bothwell was "One of the handsomest men of his time ;" "a
man generally esteemed and applauded ; the darling of the common people for his
courage and liberality, and the envy of the court." Agnes Strickland admits. "As long
as he [Bothwell] remained faithful to his duty, she [Mary] was safe." Proofs that
Bothwell was the cynosure among his peers could be piled like Pelion upon Ossa." At
quotation from Hosack must however close this note. "Bothwell was the only one
of the great nobles of Scotland, who from first to last had remained faithful to her
mother [Mary of Guise] and herself.   *   *   Whatever may have been his follies
or his crimes, *no man could say* JAMES HEPBURN *was either a hypocrite or a traitor.
Though staunch to the religion he professed he never made it the cloak* of his ambition ;
though driven into exile and reduced to extreme poverty by the malice of his enemies
he never, so far as we know, accepted of a foreign bribe. [Of what single other noble
could this be said.] In an age when political fidelity was the rarest of virtues, we
need not be surprised that his sovereign at this time trusted and rewarded him   *   *
although the common people admired his liberality and courage ('his characteristic daring'). Bothwell among his brother nobles had no friends. Why ? They
envied his gifts and more his influence with the Queen. Need any man ask a higher
eulogy than his enemies have been compelled to accord."

throw the cards away and grasp the stakes we have so subtly won.
Who can gainsay our marriage now? The high nobility have urged
me to wed thee as worthy my espousals. I agree. And now, like a
knight errant, you have borne me off, as Pluto bore to Hades Pros-
erpine. All that remains is but to wed, to wed before the world as we
were wed when first I listened to thy passion's speech and gave myself
in all, but name of wife, to thee. Carry me back to Edinburgh and
there let holy church unite us by one rite, even though it be in secret.
Then marry me in public by those forms to which you yield obedience
—forms through which neither my love nor fond caresses, nay, my high
commands could never make you break. Think you I do not honor
you for that! The man that lives up to such motto of his house,
" Kiip Trest," and cannot be induced to swerve from that at the appeal
of ambition, statescraft, nay, far more, of passion ; by the lure of the
possession of the woman ·that he loves, that woman too a queen, a
loving, lovely queen ; that is the man for me. Forgive that I have
brought you to this pass ; and triumph with me that my Lorraine blood
has loosed the knot and brought the end about; that Mary Stuart
stands before the world so low in public estimation, and so high in her
grand estimate of Bothwell, her own sore-tried lover, that she must
wed him or sink so deep that she can never rise again. Do you
imagine a woman can forget that which she bears within her bosom
or the one beloved to whom it owes allegiance. Disannul the bonds
that shackle thee before the world, never to me, and Mary will wed
thee and glory in the doing it as woman never yet before did, or will
do such deed. The tempest's passed, we have now reached our port,
let us repair the past, and in each others arms forget what is fore-
gone, and valiantly defy or trust the future. Take me—my king, my
lover, husband, all in one—into thine arms, where I should have ever
been, had I been ever bold towards thee as thou hast ever shown
thyself valiant for me and mine. (*She throws herself into the arms of*
Bothwell, *and then, after fondly caressing her, he leads her out.*)

An interval of about two weeks is supposed to elapse between Scenes
IV. and V.)

SCENE V.—*Another Apartment in the Castle of Dunbar. Time, about the 1st May,* 1567. MARY *enters, followed by* BOTHWELL *reading a despatch.*

BOTHWELL (*striking, violently, the paper which he holds*). Dearest, I learn by this despatch, sent me by one in Edinburgh in whom I place implicit trust, that those same Lords, who, at the Annesley Supper, signed the bond urging you to wed with me and pledging "their lives, their fortunes and their honors" both to sustain and maintain us twain, are plotting now, again, against us both. Who could believe that men of such high standing could be guilty of such low practices—such infamy. The ink was scarcely dry upon the "Ainslie Supper Bond" when the principal lords who signed it entered, secretly, into another Bond to oppose the execution of the plan of what they had themselves suggested. They did not even wait for the consummation of the marriage, they had so hotly urged upon their Queen, before they bonded together to render the union void and negatory. They declare, false traitors as they are, that I desire and design to gain possession of the royal infant Prince in order to make way with him, even as I murdered his father,—a crime of which they themselves acquitted me and held me scathless, pledging all that men hold dear to uphold my innocence and support my dignity. By St. Bride of Bothwell, as Hereditary Lord High Admiral of Scotland, I have fought hard to clear its seas of the vilest scum of the ocean, the pirates that infested them, but what were they to these, the very scum, although high nobles, of the Earth. They make me revolt against my own humanity that I share the form and soul of such foul miscreants like them. Bothwell! Bothwell! you never stained your escutcheon with a lie, nor took a bribe, nor swerved from loyalty, nor played the hypocrite, nor used religion to cloak hypocrisy; how? how could you imagine that there could be such utter absence of all sense of honor from the souls of prelates and of peers? Out upon it! Fight, the last dread argument and resource of kings; they want it, eh? Well, they shall have it to the bitter end.

MARY. Unworthy and faithless traitors, as they styled themselves if they could or should prove false to these pledges. Infamous wretches: liars all, all the same ilk. They are all the tribe of Judas—beginning with that miserable Darnley. Is there any truth left on earth—at least in Scotland?

BOTH. It seems not. They charge that I have violated you here on the 25th of April,—by violence possessed myself of all long since was mine through infinite love and tenderness.

MARY. Why on that day, that very day, I came personally forward and issued a special authority to accomplish your divorce and set you free to wed me ; yes, on that day, the suit of the Countess Jane was commenced before the Reformed Civil Court. When will these vilest accusations cease.

Both. I fear not till I grasp the truncheon of command, as sovereign and as consort, and set my iron heel upon the serpent's head and crush it. When that time comes, no more such ill-timed interference, sweetheart, as when you saved foul Lethington and fool Melville from my dagger's point. My love, your mercy is but weakness. For them, for men like Morton and your bastard brother, Murray, there is no safe recipes except that which Murray had for Huntley, Chastelard, John Gordon, and poor Davie—death !

Mary. I see it now ; we will yet have the heads of one and all, from the Bastard down through the whole list of falsehood ! Will we not, my Bothwell ? I will not be merciful again, my own, unless you counsel it.

Both. And when I so advise, you need not fear to pardon. We must set forth for Edinburgh, there to be married and, to avoid all future questions, by *both* rites—in private by the forms that you respect ; in public by the rites held sacred by me and by the majority of your subjects. You see the reason for all this : do you consent ?

Mary. I do, my dearest James ; your wishes are my own ; your will my law ; your thoughts my counsellors and guides ; your will my judgment. Yes, our marriage must be hurried forward. The life I bear within me must not see the light to throw discredit on its authors : *that* allows no pause. So give your orders. Whatsoe'er they be I acquiesce in everything. I know that everything you do, is not only the wisest for you and me ; my rights, our rights, and Scotland's weal.

Both. If the Fates smile upon us. *Fortuna sequatur :* if Fortune be propitious, love, we will crush out the whole brood of vipers. (*Blows a whistle. Enter* French Paris.) Bid my adjutant, Captain Blackadder, summon to the field all who acknowledge fealty to the Hepburn and feel for Mary Stuart the full devotion that they owe their Queen. (*To* Mary.) Within ten days the Courts will set me free, and then our marriage must follow most incontinent.

French Paris. Have you any further orders for your adjutant ?

Both. Stay, follow me ! It may be better to set down all things orderly in writing. The Queen and I will sign each document ; she as the source of every power and grace, and I as her Lieutenant-General.

(*Exeunt* Mary *and* Bothwell, French Paris *following*.)

Between Scenes V. and VI., an interval of several days is supposed to elapse.

Edinburgh Castle

SCENE VI.—*An open space in Edinburgh, in front of the Entrance and at the Foot of the ascent to the Castle. Time, 3d May, 1567. Groups of citizens and their wives crowd the front of the stage, engaged in animated conversation.*

A VOICE (*without*). Clear the way, they are close at hand.

MANY VOICES (*without*). God save the Queen!

(*Sound of approaching military music; drums and trumpets playing a march, rapidly approaching.*)

BOTHWELL (*without*). Cease playing! (*Music stops.*) My gallant men, throw down your lances. No faitour in Edinburgh shall have excuse to say that Bothwell brought back their sovereign liege, Queen Mary, with any show of force or aught of constraint upon her gracious will or person!

Enter MARY, *led by* BOTHWELL, *the latter richly but soberly attired in a dress trimmed with wild-cat fur. He is bareheaded, and carries his plumed bonnet in his hand. They are accompanied by the* EARL OF HUNTLEY *and suite,* CAPTAIN BLACKADDER, *Hackbutteers, Troopers dismounted, Attendants, &c. The Queen and* BOTHWELL *are preceded by trumpeters and drummers, and succeeded by soldiers and attendants. The military form in the rear of the stage and throw out guards toward the front, to keep back the crowd.*

MARY. Be covered, my dear lord; it ill befits the man who is to wed the Queen to stand uncovered in her presence. (*She playfully snatches his bonnet from his hand and places it on his head.*)

(*The populace stand silent.*)

CAPTAIN BLACKADDER (*to the crowd*). Why do you not cheer?

Have you no welcome for your Queen, and for the noble gentleman
who is to wed her.

VOICES (*in the crowd*). We have no cheers for the murderer and
murderess of Lord Darnley, our sweet King Henry, Lord Darnley.

BLACKADDER (*rushing into the crowd and striking several with the
flat of his sword*). Out caitiffs, out!   Cheer, or I will prick you
with my sword's point until you cry out something.

(*A faint, quavering, unwilling cheer is given.*)

WOMAN'S VOICE (*in the crowd*). God bless your Majesty, if you had
no art nor part in the slaying of the King, your husband.

Henry Stuart, Lord Darnley; King of Scots (murdered).
From an old print.

MARY. This is a sorry welcome for a sovereign to her capital.
What a contrast to the welcome I received on my return from France,
six years ago. And, yet, I was less happy then without you than now
with you, my Bothwell!

BOTH. Thanks, my own sweet, for that kind word and thought. The weather welcomes us, if not these caitiff burghers, on whom the sun should frown. Auspicious be the omen that its brightness floods down on us advancing to our marriage. "Happy," says the proverb, "is the bride that the sun shines on" and oh, how lovely is this month of May !

VOICE (*from the crowd*). "*Mense malas Maio nubere vulgus ait.*" Woe! woe to those who marry in the month of May!

MARY. How ominous this cry!

BOTH. Nay, love ; why pay a moment's heed to this rebellious crew. I will soon scourge them into submissive silence. (*Signs to* CAPTAIN BLACKADDER, *who goes out and returns with a body of Pikemen, who drive out the crowd, striking them over the head with the staves, and pricking them with the points of their lances.*)

BOTH. (*to the trumpeters*). Summon the Castle !

(*Flourish of trumpets. Enter from the rear* SIR JAMES BALFOUR, *Deputy-Governor of Edinburgh Castle, with his Following, through the ranks of the soldiers in the background, which open to afford him passage. He pays obeisance to the Queen and* BOTHWELL *in dumb show.*)

BOTH. (*to* MARY). Give me your hand, my love ! (*To* SIR JAMES BALFOUR.) Show us the way, my own good Sir Deputy Provost. (*To* CAPTAIN BLACKADDER.) Marshal the troops, and forward.

(CAPTAIN BLACKADDER *motions the music to move off after* SIR JAMES BALFOUR, *who passes through the Entrance Gate of the Castle, and then the troops, in the rear, face inwards and prepare to follow.*)

BOTH. Hold fast my hand, sweetheart. If we have none others with us but my brave Border Lairds and their bold followers, we have, in any event, each other. In, to the Castle ! There we are masters of this rebel town. A few short hours and the rites of both our churches shall make us one in law—as we have long been one in heart—forever and forever !

(*As they turn to go, the trumpets and drums begin to sound a triumphal march ; the Hackbutteers on the sides of the stage present arms, and then shoulder their muskets, the Troopers and Pikemen range themselves, and as the whole prepare to move, the crowd force themselves in again upon the stage wherever there is any space, and, amid martial music on the stage and a salvo of artillery from the Castle, without, the Curtain falls.*)

Borthwick Castle.

ACT V.

SCENE I.— *The beautiful and high-arched Great, or Banquetting, Hall of Borthwick Castle on the Gore.* *   Time, 7th of June, 1567; twenty-three days after the Marriage of* MARY *and* BOTHWELL.

Enter BOTHWELL *and* ORMISTON. *Both are in complete armor and carry their helmets in their hands.* BOTHWELL *strides to and fro, as if greatly exasperated.*

BOTHWELL.. Damn this surprise! It is chargeable alone to the generalship of Kirkaldy of Grange. The others had neither hearts to dare nor brains to plan it. (*Reflectingly.*) When the Queen and I left Edinburgh, the sky seemed clear; horizon free of clouds, and, now, it is

---

* "BORTHWICK CASTLE. One and a half miles north of Crichton, equidistant between Tyne Head and Fushie Bridge Station, is the ruined *Castle of Borthwick*, a massive gloomy double tower, 90 feet high, 74 feet by 68 feet broad, and encompassed by a strongly fortified court, remarkable for the excellence of its masonry and the thickness of its walls. Built in the 15th century, in form it is nothing more than the old border keep, though on a larger scale than usual. The object of the Lord of Borthwick seems to have been to have all the space and accommodation of these cluster of edifices within the four (4) walls of his simple square block, and thus this building is believed to be the largest specimen of that class of architecture in Scotland."

"THE GREAT HALL is remarkable for some very fine carving, particularly over the all clouded over with every sign of change ; impending tempest. Such is life—at all events, life in Scotland. (*To* ORMISTON.) Are you sure that we can trust our scouts, and the Castle is beset by not more than twelve hundred Border horsemen ?

ORMISTON. Perfectly sure, my Lord. They counted them when they first met under the Lords of Home and Morton. They had some seven hundred. Kirkaldy, Lindesay, assuredly, brought up not over five hundred more. This is some four or five days since. It is more likely that many of the moss-troopers have slunk off home, than that they have gained in numbers. Our scouts add, that many were unwilling to mount against your Earlship and the Queen ; but were enforced by threat of ban, outlawing, fire and halter.

BOTH. Have they any cannons ?

ORM. None.

BOTH. Many hackbutts ? (Muskets.)

ORM. The volleys that we hear show their supply of hand-cannon is most scant. Our scouts say few, and ill served at that. Home's troopers are poorly armed ; some few in steel and most in jacks. Morton's men are little better. Kirkaldy has a more trusty company.

BOTH. You are a staunch fellow, Ormiston, and fear neither man nor devil. These walls are strong and could laugh at cannon. If I leave a score of our best men, can you hold out a day or two against assault ?

---

fire-place, and a canopied niche in the side wall. Hither fled Queen Mary and Both-well, 7th June, 1567, about a month after their marriage, on the alarm of the Con-federate Lords gathering their forces against them. But they were scarce safe within the walls, when Lords Morton and Hume, with a hostile array, appeared before them. Under these circumstances Bothwell first got clear away, and afterwards Mary (in the disguise of a page) to Dunbar. *One of the rooms is still traditionally called the* QUEEN's ROOM. In November, 1650, Cromwell, annoyed by a horde of moss-trooping marauders, who had taken post in Borthwick, sent a missive to Lord Borthwick, that if he did not " Walk away, and deliver his house," he would " bend his cannon against him," a threat which proved effectual, and prevented a bombardment. The parish church, which was rebuilt in 1865, is dedicated to St. Kentigern, and has an apsidal chancel. The manse of Borthwick was the birthplace of Robertson the historian.
" MURRAY's *Hand-book for Scotland.*"

" The castle of BOTHWELL's *friend*, LORD BORTHWICK, a baronial pile of magnificent aspect and vast strength, [is] situated in a lonely but fertile glen eleven miles south of the capital [Edinburgh]. On a rocky eminence, moated around by the waters of the Gore, the Donjon Tower of Borthwick, from its base to its projecting battlements, rises to the height of more than a hundred feet, with walls sixteen feet thick. A lofty barbican, flanked by a square and round embattled towers, slit by innumerable loop-holes for arrows and musketry, together with a portcullis, double gates and draw-bridges, rendered it impregnable to the knights and horsemen of the Confederates, who were unprovided with artillery requisite for battering this stronghold, which is one of the finest examples of military architecture in Scotland ; and so grand and imposing is its aspect, that every visitor, on coming in sight of its gigantic facade, is impressed with silence and awe. " GRANT's *Kirkaldy of Grange.*"

ORM. As long as victuals last, a scum like Home's would never dare assault.

BOTH. How many troopers have I in full armor, with strong long-winded horses ?

ORM. Forty or fifty.

BOTH. Can I trust *you* to protect the Queen ?

ORM. You can trust me to the death. Do I not fight with a halter round my neck ? Did Morton, Home, or Lindesay catch me, I should have Jeddart justice—short shrift, however long the trial afterwards. (*Emphatically*.) My Lord of Bothwell, you know me.

BOTH. I do, old friend. I am resolved to sally forth, cut my way through, and raise the country. Within two days I will relieve you.

(*A volley of musketry fired without; one or two panes of glass are broken in the windows by the shots. Cries without*, Traitor ! murderer ! butcher ! Come out and maintain the challenge you offered to those who charge you with the murder of the King ! White livered hound, leave your leman ! Come out and fight, if you dare !)

BOTHWELL (*without paying the slighest attention to the musketry, but roused by these words*). Ormiston, you hear this. I'll stand it no longer. Had it not been for the Queen, I would have cut my way out at the first. The man who spoke must be right near the castle. The clearness of the words prove that. Go pick out some good shot and shoot him dead ! Get my men ready ; bring out my horse ! Be ready to throw open the gates, and drop the drawbridge ! Go ! you know your duty, go ! (*To* ORMISTON, *about to leave*.) Stay ! Dress a good tall youth in woman's garments. We'll have him in our midst, and the besetting force will think I am carrying off the Queen. If I get through, they'll think the Queen's escaped ; and either rip their horses in pursuit or scatter and draw off when they believe the prize at which they aimed has 'scaped their clutches. Either way I shall succeed. Ormiston away ; be quick ! be quick !

(*As* ORMISTON *leaves the Hall, the* QUEEN *enters from the opposite side. She is dressed as a page, booted and spurred, and carries a riding whip in her hand.*)

BOTH. What means this dress, sweet one ?

MARY. To ride forth with you. Have I not often said I wished I was a man to sleep in field, under the open sky, and be a trooper like my hero ?

BOTH. (*embracing her*). Love, it would never do. Your pages jerkin would scarcely bide a shot, and poorest lance would run you through and through. (*Holding her at arms length and gazing at her with admiration.*) My own brave Mary, be patient ! Trust Ormiston, and by

St. Bride of Bothwell within two days I will be back and blow off
Home's and Morton's riff-raff like chaff.

(*Several musket-shots discharged overhead, and then a saker [small
piece of artillery, 5¼ pdr. gun], followed by shouts of triumph within
the Castle, and cries of dismay and horror without.* BOTHWELL *rushes
towards the window to observe thence what has occurred.* MARY *restrains
him.*)

MARY. My soul, my very life; be not so venturesome! At least
put on your helmet. A stray shot might take the life which is my life.

ORM. (*runs in hastily, laughing*). My Lord, the men about us are
the veriest cowards. The boasting blackguard, we heard just now a-
railing, was hid in some tall gorse within long bow-shot, and in a hollow just beyond a dozen more lay hiding. We shot the fellow and, as
the rest ran off, the saker killed another. (*Laughs immoderately.*) This
startled the whole hive, and far and near you never saw such mounting
and such flighting. They spurred and galloped as if they thought
Mons-Meg was here from Edinburgh and going to open on them, and
blow them over the Cheviots. Now, if ever, is the time to mount and
sally.

BOTH. Let the men mount! (*Exit* ORMISTON.—BOTHWELL *presses*
MARY *to his breast and kisses her passionately, then clasps on his helmet and rushes toward the door. As he reaches it he pauses.*) At midnight I shall be at the Black Castle, at Cakermuir. 'Tis only two miles
distant. Fare thee well! (*Exit.*)

MARY. My own brave Bothwell! (*Looks after him with an eager
passionate gaze.*) At the Black Castle! Cakermuir! I know the
place.

(*Loud sound of the trampling of horses below. Then the clang of
heavy gates thrown open violently, followed by the rattling of chains,
and heavy fall of the drawbridge. Renewed trampling of horses, at
first below, and then without. Shouts of "A Bothwell! A Bothwell!
St. Bride for Bothwell!" The trampling of the horses and shouts
recede. Distant musketry shots.*)

MARY (*rushes to the window and looks out*). My hero! not a man
stands before him. They run like sheep chased by a wolf. Oh, that
I were a man! Oh, that I were *such* a man! My own brave husband!
(*Scene closes before her.*)

Between Scenes I. *and* II. *nine or ten hours are supposed to elapse.*

SCENE II.— *The open Moor near the Black Castle, at Cakermuir. Time, towards daylight, 8th June,* 1567. BOTHWELL, *still in armor, is discovered whispering with* HAY OF TALLA. *Several troopers lie sleeping about with their lances piled. Another trooper, leaning on his lance, stands a sentinel at one side in the back-ground.*

BOTHWELL. How we scattered Home's and Morton's rabble. The coward scum ! Thanks, brave Hay, for the stout troop you brought me. It is a darksome night. Can you make out a single light in Borthwick Castle ?

HAY OF TALLA. No, not one.   (*Enter* HEPBURN, *hastily.*)

HEPBURN. My Lord, I've seen a ghost, or else a spy, a minute or two since. Whether one or t'other it is all the same to Hepburn.

BOTH. A ghost ! A spy ! How ? Where ?

HEP. All of a sudden, looking towards Borthwick, a meteor flashed across the sky and by its glare, against a gorsey slope, I caught a glimpse of a horseman riding slowly, as if he had missed his way.

BOTH. How far away ?

HEP. Perhaps a musket shot, not more.

BOTH. Off ! Take half a dozen men and bring him in !

(*A horse neighs without, close at hand. A sentinel challenges with. out, followed by a Hurrah ! And* MARY *enters, clad as in the preceding scene of this Act, followed by a group of astonished spearsmen.*)

BOTH. Gracious God ! My wife ! (*Throwing himself on his knee as* MARY *advances, catching her extended hand and covering it with kisses ; then rising and clasping her in his arms.*)   Blessed be St. Bride ! Whence came you ? How love, how ?

MARY. After you galloped forth, my husband, the rebels seemed all in confusion. At first, from the battlements, we could see them riding off by scores and troops and hundreds, some in your track, some following other courses ; until, at sunset, not a man could be discerned ; and Bothwell and Ormiston sending forth some scouts, found all were gone. I wanted him to let me go forth, but he would not. He said that you had trusted him to guard me safe in Borthwick, until you relieved us. With you went forth my life. I could not stay cooped up there like a bird in a narrow cage, while you, my husband, was in the field. So I sat me down and wrote to Sir James Balfour of Pittendriech, your Deputy and Governor of Edinburgh Castle, ordering him to hold out stoutly for me ; and to fire on the rebel Lords, if they attempted to quarter in the town. Vilest scum ! no sooner were we married as they willed, than they began again to plot and plan and Bond against us. At the same time I wrote to the French Ambassador Du Croc, to see these Lords, and learn their real purposes. These orders I sent off by the young Laird of Reres. By this time it was night. When all was quiet I stole down from my chamber, gliding like a ghost into the banquetting hall, and by a cord let myself down from the window to the moat.

Borthwick Castle.

BOTH. My God! 'Tis some thirty feet: bravest of women! (*His armor rattling with his agitation.*) Whence was derived such courage, then ?

MARY. It seemed like nothing. Was I not flying to my Lord, my husband ? Did I not know where to find him ? Here!

BOTH. But where did you obtain a horse ?

MARY. 'Love laughs at locksmiths,' says the proverb, darling, and gold builds a bridge across the widest stream. Two of my women helped to lower me from the window. As expected, the postern stood unlocked by that same golden key. Then I scrambled through the moat, and up the grassy counterscarp, on, into the open ground. Thus, my Bothwell, I found myself beyond the ditch and there, close by it, a close-cropped nag, bridled and saddled, held by a faithful groom of low degree. We'll raise him up, my Bothwell, and fill his pouch with Mary Reals (or Cruickston Dollars). I knew the country well, and while the light lasted, marked well the direction of the Black Castle you had mentioned as you parted. Crichton Muir was no strange place to me.

Have I not galloped over it, hawking, with you beside me, husband, when I but little dreamed we ever should be man and wife.

Both. But the night has been very dark.

Mary. Husband, you forget the glowworms; the Muir is famous for them at this season. The gorse was all aflame with those stars of the green earth !

Both. Bravest of women, and you encountered no one ?

Mary. Not a shadow crossed my path, and if aught did (*laughing merrily*), did I not have my sword, and have I not ridden like a trooper with pistols in my holsters, and am I not Bothwell's love and wife, and (*drawing herself up proudly*) am I not Mary Stuart, Queen of Scotland ?

Both. God's blessing upon thee, best and bravest woman ! (*Clasps her in his arms.*) And now to horse, we must breakfast in Dunbar. (*To* Hepburn.) There is no longer need of secrecy. Have I not here my dearest and my Queen ? The country is alive with friends. Lords Seton, Yestor and Borthwick, together with the Lairds of Walkton, Bass, Black Ormiston of that Ilk, and he of Lothian, Wedderburn, Blackadder and Laughton, are all in saddle, gathering to my standard. The Border Bonnet Lairds, with every man that they can raise are spurring to Dunbar. Morton and Home with their whole rebel force following, have ridden fast as nags can carry them to Edinburgh. Sound trumpet ! Sound to horse ! Blow merrily ! To horse ! To horse ! To horse ! On to Dunbar !

Ruins of Dunbar Castle.

(*Trumpet sounds "Boots and Saddles." The call is repeated from point to point without. Finally the different trumpeters unite in a triumphant Fanfare, amid which the scene closes in front of them.*)

Six days are supposed to elapse between Scenes II. *and* III.

SCENE III.—Lethington's *chambers in Edinburgh.* Lethington *enters reading a despatch;* Morton *meeting, interrupts him.*

Morton. Maitland, you do not believe in God! You must perforce believe in the devil ; for never was a plot concocted with human cunning and wickedness, such as ours, that could have succeeded without the help of Auld Hornie himself. Do you remember our first

DEATH of RIZZIO.

(From an old engraving.)

conference in my chambers, shortly after Mary Stuart's marriage ? To complete the split between the Queen and Darnley, we had to bring the silly long laddie to believe in Rizzio's intimacy with his wife. The Italian was disposed of. He troubled us no more.

LETHINGTON. True ! That was sagaciously accomplished and converted the Queen's disgust for her faithless, brutal, cowardly consort,
into that positive hatred that sprung the mine at Kirk-o'-Field.

MOR. (*with a subdued laugh*). How the dolt walked into the toils !
No silly rabbit was ever toled by a turnip into a trap more easily
(*Laughs.*) Darnley traveled to his death as complacently as a cosset
lamb is led in to the shambles.

LETH. Who could have believed that "Gloriosus" Bothwell could
be brought to serve our purposes so perfectly. And, yet, it is not so
wonderful. Loyal, himself, he cannot see into the depths of our dis-
loyalty to everything but our own interests. We understand each
other. He comprehends nothing beyond his love for Mary and his
hopes for Scotland. He seeks to rule the realm, not for his own advantage, but for the welfare of the people, the glory of the Queen, and
his own credit—without a party too, by his own bravery ; the honest
fool ! Countries are not ruled so—men cannot rule except through parties, partisans and passion. His affection for the Queen was of such
sterling stuff, that it even stood the test of her injustice, and her sudden, unrestrained longing for a far lesser man. Think you, he would
have stood the arrogance of Murray had he not loved the Queen in
spite of every wrong ?

MOR. Justly are you styled the Chameleon. You change with
every phase of circumstance. Were you not caught by Mary ?

LETH. (*drawing himself up*). That is my own concern, Earl Morton. Let alone my personal affairs ! Let us resume our business.
Darnley dead, Bothwell acquitted and married to the Queen, our pear
is ripe, and ready to drop into our hands. This requires but a breath
of popular opinion. How I scorn the popular thought and voice ! Popular opinion, forsooth ; the first so easily misled, the second roused to
fury by such little cause or without right. "The 'generous people' (*sarcastically*), so much more capable of what may be called the poetry of
sentiment than of true feeling." Through it we are masters of the capital. The vast majority believe that Bothwell seeks possession of the
Royal infant, Mary's child by Darnley, or perhaps by Davie—who
knows that—to rid himself of him as he and we rid both of the child's
father. Now, away with him ! Away with Mary ! Murray becomes
Regent. He, again, is but a tool ; and all Scotland from the Clyde unto
the Shetlands is ours, ours, all ours !

MOR. And, yet, it seems that we must fight for it, and that God
which you deny has shown himself throughout all time, The Lord of
Hosts and God of Battles.

LETH. Tush, Morton ! With all your worldly sense and knowledge
of mankind, you cannot get rid of the old religious leaven, the seed

sown at your mother's knee and fostered by John Knox. Did not John Knox advise the death of Rizzio, connive at murder, thunder from the pulpit against the Papist Darnley and the Pope's agent Rizzio? Priest and minister, they are alike, and selfish interest is the hand that guides. The Queen is fickle. With legal right and sole possession will come satiety. I know her thoroughly. Her passion sated for the nonce, she must be made to separate from Bothwell and trust in us.

MOR. This seems past hope! We thought we had her when she and he were caught in Borthwick Castle; and yet he cut his way out like a brave fellow as he is, and she, apparelled as a trooper, booted and spurred, straddling her saddle like a man, stole forth and joined her lover-husband, fled to him as when he lay wounded at the Hermitage, as the old song runs—

> "Some mair about the Queene is saed,
> And how ye Earle got wounded :
> How she, towards him, to see him fledde—
> The which she very soon did."

Hermitage Castle.

LETH. Love thrives on opposition in a wayward, imperious woman. Kirkaldy, with all his boasted chivalry, is playing around the bait of this Scotch siren. We must so pitch the hook that it catches in his gills. The Queen believes that he is honest; that if she but accepts him as a pilot for the time, and furls her sails, she can bid defiance to the squall, and with serener weather take Bothwell to her arms again, as captain, and sail on with him in peace. (*Trumpet without.*) She was grievously mistaken in Darnley, but she errs more fatally in her judgment of Kirkaldy. We must keep in with him, for now he looms up as our decoy to win her confidence from Bothwell, as the farmer's use a tulchan-calf to induce a cow which has lost her young to let down her milk. With all his gilt of chivalry, Kirkaldy has his price, and can play knight or knave, patriot or informer, good friend or spy, as the wind sets and his purpose jumps. John Knox knew his real nature. Kirkaldy, if not a murderer in fact, is a murderer at heart, as cold-blooded as any of the worst of our party. But— hark! (*A trumpet sounds without.*)

MOR. That does not sound like peace. (*Opening the window and leaning out*). Ho, sir! What are the news?

VOICE (*without*). The army of the Queen is marching upon Edinburgh. Our scouts have brought the news that their light-horse have been already discovered from the platform of the Castle.

MOR. (*to the speaker, without*). Thanks, friend! (*Shutting the window and turning to* LETHINGTON.) This looks very much like a fight, and the chances are not in our favor, certainly not the right. (*Sarcastically.*) Remember the Round-about-Raid!

LETH.* One of the wise captains of antiquity, on being told that the enemy were advancing and were determined to fight, replied, "That will be just as we may choose." The man was a great general. We must show wise leaders still are living. There will be no fight, Earl Morton; you play at whist! Who understands the game and holds the leading trumps and strongest cards must win, unless he throws his luck away. Kirkaldy is the winning trump this time, and I can play him. We must take the saddle. Be calm and trust in me! I tell you, Kirk- aldy is our winning card, and he is in my hand.   (*Exit.*)

MORTON (*lingers in deep thought. Cannon shot without*). Ha! What does that mean? Can it be Balfour, from the castle, firing on the city!

    Off, Morton, off! Matters brook no delay:
    Bothwell or I must conquer Scotland's sway!

Scene closes as near as possible to the front, so as to afford space and opportunity to arrange Scene IV. *behind it.*

Forty-eight hours are supposed to elapse between Scenes III. *and* IV.

---

* No likeness of this Maitland (the younger) of Lethington could be obtained for this play which was sharp enough to be reproduced by photo-engraving for printing. No portrait of Kirkaldy of Grange is known to exist.

Mary Stuart, Queen of Scots.
From the famous portrait in the gallery of the Hermitage Palace, St. Petersburgh, Russia.
Originally in Paris, France, prior to the great French Revolution.

Demi-Lancer, Trooper in puffed and ribbed armor and Yeoman of the Guard.
Middle of the XVI. Century.

SCENE IV.—*Carberry Hill.**   *Time, Afternoon of 15th June, 1567.*
*A knoll, whence the prospect extends to the westward and northward,
looking over the nearer lines of the Queen's forces, and toward
those, beyond, of the Confederate Lords.   In the immediate rear*

---

* The Confederates [Rebels] marched eastward against [Dunbar], from which
Mary had issued her proclamation for mustering an army in defence of her person. It
was not obeyed save by Bothwell's immediate allies, by whose exertions the Queen
soon beheld four thousand brave men of Lothian and the Merse arrayed under her
standard. Bothwell had a guard, or chosen band, of two hundred [hackbutteers or]
harquebussiers and the royal stores at Dunbar furnished his troops with falcons, or light
[6 pdr.] field-pieces. While her forces were rapidly increasing, the Queen marched to
Glademuir, and occupied the lofty tower of Seatoun ; her soldiers were meantime can-
toned in the adjacent villages of Preston, Tranent and Cockenzie. After halting for a
night at Musselburg, the Confederates, as they marched out of that ancient and picturesque little town, with trumpets sounding and kettle-drums beating, amid the clamor
of the inhabitants and the tolling of bells, learned that the forces of Mary, led by the
Duke of Orkney, were in position on the HILL OF CARBERRY, an eminence above the
town, commanding an extensive prospect of the sea and surrounding country. On the
summit of that hill, now known as the QUEEN'S SEAT, Mary held with Sir William
Kirkaldy that conference which was to have so much influence on her future destiny.
It is now covered with the richest copsewood : *then it was bleak and bare,* or studded

stand three pieces of artillery (falcons or 6 pdrs.), pointed at the latter, with a few " Constables" in charge: of whom one, assigned to each gun, at intervals waves his linstock to keep the slow-match alight and ready for immediate use. Near these are groups of

only by the tufts of dark evergreen whin [furze, gorse] or the golden bells of the yellow broom ; and *a rough block of stone on its summit formed a seat for the unfortunate* MARY.

It was the morning of Sunday the 15th of June [1567] ; the weather was intensely hot, and the troops of both factions suffered considerable annoyance from the clouds of dust, the closeness of the atmosphere, and the burning rays of the unclouded sun, which darted on their *shining armor.* Bothwell—or the Duke of Orkney—commanded the whole of Mary's little force, having under him the Lords Seatoun, Yester and Borthwick, with four Barons of the Merse—viz., Wedderburn, Langton, Cumledge and Hirsel ; and those of the Bass, Waughton, Ormiston in Lothian, and Ormiston of that Ilk, in Teviotdale, all men of courage and high descent.

The Confederates were formed in two columns : Alexander, Lord Home and the Earl of Morton led the first, and Athol the second, with Glencairn, Ruthven, Semphill and Sanquhar. Kirkaldy, with his two hundred spears, had galloped eastward, to get in between Bothwell and the Castle of Dunbar, hoping to cut off his retreat, and by a sudden charge break the array of his cannoneers.

The main body of the Confederates were drawn up with their left flank to the sea, almost on the same ground which, twenty years before, had witnessed the unfortunate Battle of Pinkie. On both sides the numbers were now nearly equal, but they differed greatly in discipline.

The army of Mary consisted of a hastily-mustered and inexperienced multitude, while that of the Confederates was principally composed of gentlemen [perjured villians of high birth, renowned for courage, and brave as they were determined].

The ground where those adverse bands drew up for battle is now covered with groves of the most luxuriant wood and studded with modern villas. In those days it ex-hibited but two solitary shepherds' huts and Pinkie Burn winding between banks of willows, sedges and reeds ; the old taper spire of St. Michael's Kirk, an edifice of unknown antiquity, built of stone squared by Roman hands, rose on the Mount of the Prætorium above the wooded banks of the Esk ; which, after making a beautiful sweep around it, and passing under the steep old Roman bridge of three arches, which, a thousand years before, had connected the Castrum with the Municipium, flows into the Forth between Fisherrow and Musselburgh. The latter was then, as now, a strag-gling and irregular burgh, with gable-ended streets, by the ruined chapel of Lorretto, and the tall old manor-house of Pinkie, with its picturesque turrets overtopping its dark and shadowy groves. It was then the residence of Kirkaldy's foeman, Durie of that Ilk, Abbot of Dunfermline, who, prior to the Reformation, had been Lord Su-perior of Musselburgh. Such was the prospect from the hill—

> " Where Mary agonizéd stood,
>   And saw contending hosts below
> Press forward to the deadly feud.
> With hilt to hilt, and hand to hand,
> The children of our mother land
>   For battle met ! The banners flaunted
> Amid Carberry's beechen grove ;
> And kinsmen braving kinsmen strove
>   Undaunting and undaunted."—

royal, regular Hackbutteers, belonging to the Queen's body-guard, at ease, and parties of Border noblemen and their retainers, Jack. men, evidently as if just dismounted, and leaning on their long spears. In the front centre are MARY STUART *and* BOTHWELL ; *and, to the right, but withdrawn a space,* KIRKALDY OF GRANGE. *Behind the Queen is* CAPTAIN BLACKADDER, *one of* BOTHWELL'S *subordinates, watching what is occurring in the enemy's ranks and his remarks serve as an explanation or* CHORUS.

BLACKADDER (*to* BOTHWELL). Hasten, my Lord, your colloquy: the foe
    Are striving to outflank us. Look, their horse
    To close the road to Dunbar, headlong spur.
    If fight 's the word, now is the time to fight,
    Lest we both lose advantage of the sun
    Full in their faces ; our position too ;
    And worst, if beaten, our retreat 's cut off.
(*Finding* BOTHWELL *does not pay immediate attention, raising his voice.*)
    Mighty earl, great Captain ! Here we stand not
    To hear the nightingale's sweet am'rous notes,
    But hearken to the trumpet's points of war—
    Then bid them sound ! Shoot falcons and set on !

An ancient trench, which had been formed by the English in 1547, lay before the line of Mary's forces ; and on the summit of this Bothwell, gallantly arrayed in brilliant armor, "showed himself, mounted on a brave steed." *He was well known to be an accomplished knight and fearless horseman.* * * If anything could have retrieved her affairs at this desperate crisis, it must have been a headlong advance under cover of a cannonade ; and Bothwell should have instantly led on the soldiers of Mary to victory or death ; instead of which, while anxiously awaiting the arrival of Lord Her- ries and others with reinforcements, he suffered an ineffectual negotiation to take place by means of the French ambassador. * * *

"We came not to this field," sternly added Alexander, Earl of Glencairn, "to ask pardon for what we have done, but to yield it unto those who have offended !" Du Crocq, finding it vain to expect an accommodation with such intractable spirits, bade adieu to the queen, and with his train departed for Edinburgh.

Alive to the perils of her situation, the unhappy Queen saw fully the manifold dangers which environed her. * * On her palfry she rode through the ranks of her little host, but found the soldiers dispirited, fatigued and viewing her coldly. Many, who were overcome by the heat of the weather, stole from their places to quench their thirst in Pinkie Burn, but forgot to rejoin their colors; others de- serted openly in bands, and none appeared to remain staunch to her but Bothwell's band of Harquebussiers, and the immediate vassals of the House of Hepburn. It was at this crisis that Kirkaldy's squadron, after encompassing the hill, halted ; when Bothwell, perceiving his flank turned, and matters becoming desperate, sent down a herald-at-arms with a gauntlet of defiance, offering by a single combat to prove his innocence of King Henry's murder. GRANT'S *"Kirkaldy of Grange."*

MARY (*continuing a conversation which had been going on before the scene opened*). I am resolved to trust Kirkaldy—

BOTHWELL. Ah !

What glamour blinds thee, love ? Thou know'st him not :
The hireling spy and England's trait'rous tool.
He but deceives thee, with his specious tale ;
His boasted chivalry 'tis mere lacker.
Beneath the semblance of the golden truth
Is falsehood's foul and cheap-jack metal. Think
Ere you commit your fortune to such crew.

Archers. Pikemen, Border-troopers and Arquebussiers or Hackbutteers (Musketeers).
Middle of the XVI. Century.

(BOTHWELL *breaks off suddenly, rushes to a Hackbutteer, and, by signs and words inaudible to the spectators, directs him to shoot Kirkaldy, who, shading his eyes against the declining sun, is looking in a different direction towards his own friends.* MARY, *moved by* BOTHWELL'S *charges, seems lost for a moment in deep thought ; then suddenly perceives* BOTHWELL'S *intention and throws herself between the musketeer and his aim.*)

MARY. What would'st thou do ?

BOTH. Slay the deceiving villain
Who has infatuated you.

BLACKADDER (*plucking at* BOTHWELL'S *gauntlet and striving to attract the Earl's attention and addressing him, half-aside*). She's fey!
That is the the truest word you ever spoke:
My Lord! I've heard of bogles, and such like de'ils
Which borrow women's forms to ruin men—
I've followed you, thro' thick and thin, my Lord!
With dog's unquestioning fidelity;
Wages but little save the fame and game—
Which I discern that we have played and lost.
This Queen, for whom you've ventur'd life and soul,
Honors and lands, all thou hast heir'd and won,
This Mary Stuart is just such a de'il
As I have heard describ'd by Master Knox.
She's taken with a sudden frenzy for this Grange,
And like a thunderstorm, that's fierce but short,
Will damage do as big as autumn storm.
She's kindled him with lightning of her eyes,
And his responsive, flaming, flash to hers
With what belongs to you and no one else.
Think but of yourself, my Lord! Let's away
Whilst chance there is, this most mischanceful day.

MARY (*discerning that* BOTHWELL *is making up his mind to attack* KIRKALDY.)
He's under safeguard of my queenly word,
And, though he were the very knave thou say'st,
He must not die by an assassin shot.

BOTH. (*with difficulty restraining himself, and making a gesture to the musketeer to "recover arms," returns to the Queen's side*).
My love, my food, my sweetheart and my life,
Thy noble nature and thy native sense
Are both the victims of this knave's device.
Is it not better, here upon this field,
To strike one blow for honor and thy crown
Than thus abase thyself to traitors—yield
Thy freedom, and perchance thy life, to those
Who never yet have kept a single Bond
Beyond the signing, had their purposes
But borne their fruit perfidious. Hast thou not
Prov'd me, as woman never yet prov'd man
Or had the chance to do 't? Have I not shown,
By ev'ry thought, word, act, since manhood's dawn,
That Truth and Bothwell were synonymous?
"Klip Trest!" my motto—emblem of mine life.

Was I not faithful to thy mother; then
With equal truth did I not turn to thee:
Until thy love, enkindled at my own,
Or my big love, inflam'd by thy bright eyes,
Converted me from loyalty to love ?
Have I e'er fail'd thee ?   Have I not been truth,
Love, faith, devotion : *all* thy sex can ask ?
And yet thou dost not trust me : but prefer'st
The specious promise of a hireling tongue ?

MARY.   I am resolved to trust the Bonded Lords ;
Not, that I have lost faith in thee, my own,
But 'cause 't would seem as if by Fate impell'd,
This is the wisest course and fits the time.
Look but around !   Fighting is madness now.
Our army's gone to water save some few
Brave Border Jackmen and the Hackbutteers :
Besides some sixty Lairds and henchmen true,
The Constables, and our own following—
Our body guard, some cannoneers and spears—
The whole array's disbanded.   There's nothing left !
My own dear life, so that I *can* save you
All's sav'd, I hold's worth saving, here, on earth.
Do you believe that with the life you've given,
Pulsating in my bosom, I could say
Leave me an hour, did I not firmly think
That a short space would bring you back again :
Did I not *so* believe, I swear, my James !
I would far rather perish here, at once,
In very desperation, than say, Go !
A brief, sad parting and a better meeting
May bring again a long and halcyon term.

BOTH.   No, no !   No, no !   I tell thee, No !   'T would seem
As if, on board a stout, still lusty, frigate,
Because 't is slightly shatter'd by a squall,
Thou would'st abandon ship and practic'd captain,
To trust a pirate's skiff to save from storm
That lowers, but has not burst.   Oh ! Mary,
Dost thou love me ?

MARY.   My acts are the best answer.
I have gone through too much for thee to doubt it.
Oh, what have I not done to prove my love ?
-          Oh, what have I not suffer'd to be thine ?   (*Wringing her hands.*)

BOTH.   Then, by the tie united us when twain,

And by the two church rites that made us one,
I do conjure thee, let me fight this day :
Not like a felon bid me steal away.
Never before has Bothwell quit the field,
But all victorious or upon his shield.

(BOTHWELL *takes* MARY'S *hand in his, and they stand thus, grasping each others hands, for some minutes ; then clasp each other in a sad but fierce embrace.* He *glues his lips to hers, then suddenly releases her and, gazing, seems to discern that neither kisses nor caresses have changed her resolution. His eyes question her.*)

MARY (*suddenly*).   I am resolv'd to keep my word to Grange.
BOTH.   Oh, love ! my life !
MARY (*with a sad smile.*)   Alas ! we here must part ;
    Part for a time, assur'd of future meeting.
BOTH.   Wilt thou be true to me and keep thy promise,
    So often sealed with kisses, e'en beside
    The dead man's corse ; to ne'er even in thought,
    Nor word, nor bond, nor deed, annul nor weaken it ;
    Be my own Mary, till the whelming sea
    Or the cold earth put seal to either life ?
MARY.   I promise.   Go !   Before it is too late,
    Take horse for Dunbar, ere the foemen's horse
    Out in and make escape impossible.
BOTH.   Oh, woman !   Woman, what art thou but guile ?
    'Tis as I feared ; the woman is bewitch'd.
    No sooner were we married than I saw
    That she resisted—as a restive horse
    Rebels against the curb—against the tie
    That made her wife and leash'd her to a mate.
    Alas ! alas ! a sudden, frenzied spasm
    Sets her on fire with passion for this knight ;
    An overmast'ring passion.   Was I wrong
    To be so jealous, and to guard myself
    Against a change ; dishonor to my bed ?
    Let the world talk, my duty I have done
    And all is lost that I, so hardly, won.
    Still midst thy weakness Bothwell will be strong,
    My brilliant constancy shall luminate
    The blackness of thy mind's eclipse ;
    Yes, light our future if the Fates permit.
    I lov'd thee queen and woman, as a man
    And knight should love.   Fate must the Problem solve ;

This I do feel whatever ill befalls us
All who conspir'd to our separation
Will perish in their prime, ay, even when
Their fingers grasp the prize for which they sold
Their lives, their souls, their honors.   Now, farewell !
My heart is thine forever.   With Bothwell,
Arm'd at thy side, thou wer't a queen supreme.
Betrayer and betrayed ; be false to me
And set thy fame and fortune both alike.
Calvin was right, who said, "who damn'd will be,
Will be !"   Fair woman, whom, accosted, straight
I won ; I saw you, and you conquer'd me :
As a slave led me, as Cleopatra
Led Antony: and now when all our future
Hangs on decision, you, the boldest, blench
And yield.   Strike but one blow for victory !
For God's sake, Love's sake, let me strike one blow.
(*Pauses for a reply, then, with desperation.*)
Will you not fight, or let us fight ?

MARY.   Too late ! *

---

* Almost every writer who has written upon this epoch, as well as readers of the narratives of these events, have concluded that, because there was neither manœuvering nor fighting at Carberry Hill, Bothwell displayed no ability as a commander nor manhood as an individual. The French ambassador's testimony is sufficient to prove his aptness as a general, and Mary forbade any action which could demonstrate that he was not a thorough soldier.

The absolute contrary of the general calumny is the truth. All that a captain and warrior could do he did, and endeavored to do. Mary was the sole cause of his and her disasters. She insisted on hurrying to meet her enemies, when the simple delay of a few days would have ruined them; and then, when audacious-promptness was the requisite of the moment and would have condoned the previous error of mistaken impulse, she wavered, and let the chance go by. Mary has been almost invariably credited with good sense. She did not possess it; smartness she did. Whenever she undertook grand or efficient measures she fell below the occasion and manifested no sense. At Langside—as frequently referred to—her defeat was due as much to her own decision and indecision as to the selfish intentions and evil counsels of others.

As everywhere else, when called upon to display combined courage and discretion, she betrayed herself. As it was in her operations against Huntley, in 1562, so it was on Sunday, 15th June, 1567; so it was in her resolution to take refuge in England. When she permitted Bothwell to have his own way, as she did during the " Run-about-raid " and after Rizzio's murder, all went admirably, and she was triumphant whenever Bothwell's counsels were implicitly followed. The " Great Earl's " Russo-German champion, Petrick, justly observes, " The facts are manifoldly [and manifestly] distorted; they envelop Bothwell, like the opaque mists evoked by a magician, and in them this important personage again sinks into deep obscurity."

At Carberry Hill, she alone betrayed herself, her husband, and the friends of both. At Langside, she again both betrayed herself and was betrayed. Stevenson and Nau express this : " During the Queen's stay at Hamilton many difficulties arose among the lords and the other leading men of her court. In the opinion of many it was

(BOTHWELL *seizes her in his arms and kisses her wildly; but, seeing that even in this supreme moment* ρhe *makes a motion for* KIRKALDY *to approach, he suddenly releases her and strides to the left of the stage; then turns,- and perceives that* KIRKALDY *has drawn nearer to the Queen. Some one in the rear has given a signal to the enemy, and without, to the right, arise shouts, fanfares of trumpets and triumphant flams of drums.*)

BOTH. (*with concentrated bitterness*). *Varium et mutabile semper*
  Fœmina! Thus sang the Mantuan Bard.
  With truth outlives the bush that furnished bays.
  And for this fickle creature I have lost
  Country and honor—all a man holds dear.
  Oh! cruel Fortune. I have lov'd, have lost!
  All! all is lost! I am a wretch indeed.
 (*Wrings his gauntletted hands, then lets them fall disconsolately. Suddenly rousing himself, and speaking to those without.*)
  Ho! To horse! To horse!

Arms and Armor. Middle of the XVI. Century.

---

inexpedient that ρhe should remain in the hands of the Hamiltons. *Not only was the personal safety of her majesty compromised hereby, but further, many persons who*

MARY (*giving her hand to* KIRKALDY).   Come, Sir, let us go !

(*These two last exclamations are simultaneous as the curtain falls.
Rude, loud, triumphant music accompanies its descent, which gradually
changes into softer and mournful notes, as the curtain again rises upon
a double scene.*)

FOTHERINGAY.	DRAGSHOLM.
Mary, with her head on the block, the executioner standing over her with uplifted axe.	Bothwell lying dead upon the floor of his prison in Adelsborg Castle,* Denmark.

*Curtain falls again to sad music, which gradually changes into a
Symphony, as it rises on the reunion of* MARY *and*
BOTHWELL *in another sphere.*

---

were at enmity with that house refused to join her." [Burton (IV. 372.) adds, "The
Hamiltons have been blamed in recommending it [the march which involved a battle]
with *a treacherous purpose.*"] " Hercupon it was decided that she should retire to Dum-
barton, where every one could have free access to her." Langside interposed !

* " We may add," Lord Mahon goes on to say, "we have doubts whether Bothwell's
confinement in Denmark was so strict and rigorous as most histories allege. ' Such a
statement appears scarcely compatible with the following expressions of a letter from
Queen Elizabeth to the King of Denmark, in 1570."—(*Translation from the Latin.*)
" Concering Bothwell, we have certainly written at previous dates to your Serene Highness, as the undoubted murderer of his King.   [Here, Elizabeth, in her thirst for Bothwell's blood, accords the title of King to Darnley, which she consistently denied to him
while alive.]   *   *   *   wherefore, to sum up, we trust (which, nevertheless, we
have besought of your Serene Highness again and again), that the associate in a deed of
turpitude, may be confined in a dungeon and in chains in one of your state-prisons, or
certainly, as we would prefer and rather beg that he should be taken from his dungeon
to undergo trial for his crime in that place (before such tribunal), whither such admitted
wickedness should be transferred, for neither, assuredly, is it honorable for the King
[Frederick] that the murderer of a King [Darnley] should be permitted to move about
freely, without restraint (or genteely), and live without any punishment."

KIRKALDY OF GRANGE.

"That a career so honorable [as that of Kirkaldy of Grange] should have closed in shame and disgrace is one of those anomalies in human history of which it is rarely possible to offer any adequate explanation. When the hope of the defeated [Queen's] party had become desperate; when Elizabeth had shown publicly her determination that the Catholics should never triumph in Scotland; when everything which he most desired had been obtained, and what he most hated was lying prostrate and disarmed, suddenly,—with what motive who can tell,—he changed sides, became the champion of the Queen, whom he had assisted to dethrone; the enemy of the Kirk, of which he still continued a professed member: and after having filled Scotland for four years with a horrible war in a desperate cause; after involving himself in miserable intrigues with the French and the Spaniards to destroy Elizabeth, and make Mary Stuart Queen of England—that very Mary Stuart *whose fiercest accuser he himself had been, and whom he never, even after he had become her champion, professed to acquit of the crimes with which he had charged her*—he closed this shameful palinodia [recantation] of a once honorable life where alone, as now we see it, it was possible for such a course to end—on the gallows. No one will call in question the justice of his end who is acquainted with the detail of the war for which he was responsible; but of the motives which could have induced him to follow a course so unlike himself, so inherently disgraceful, and so desperate in its chances of success, no historian that we know of has offered so much as an attempt at explanation."—*Fraser's Magazine*, Vol. 47, p. 535.

BOTHWELL'S ADVANTAGES.

Teulet, in his Preface, xxi., says that, besides the Casket Letters, a multitude of contemporaneous documents prove the violent, boundless passion of Mary for Bothwell, who possessed all the physical advantages proper to seduce a young woman, and was only a few years older than the Queen; since, when they were married, in 1567 (15th May), he was about thirty, and Mary (born 5th December, 1542) was twenty-five years and five months old.

ERRATA.

Page 27, 28. "Guistizia," should read: Giustizia.
" 26, second line. For "e're, read: o'er.
" 45, third line. Should read: *per fas et nefas.*
" 46, fortieth line. For "indeed no!" read: indeed, none!
" 55, sixteenth line. For "negatory," read: nugatory.
" 56, twenty-eighth line. Before "wisest," insert: best but the.
" 64, thirty-first line. For "Bothwell," read: Borthwick.
" 64, thirty-sixth line. For "Pittendriech," read: Pittendreich.

Appendix—Notes.

Note I. to Act III., Scene III.—The Casket Letters, Sonnets, &c.

"Harpagon.—Et cette Cassette comment est elle faite ?"
"Maître Jacques.— . . . . . Elle est petite, si on le veut prendre par là ;
mais je l'appelle grande pour ce qu' elle contient."   Molière.

Although the famous Casket Letters, Sonnets, &c., from Mary
to Bothwell are not mentioned in this Drama, because they were only
discovered after the date of its action, ending with their separation at
Carberry Hill, they must receive some notice, since the spirit and sen-
timents evident and expressed in them, are embodied in the conversa-
tions between Mary and Bothwell in the play. That these letters, &c.,
are genuine, the writer, after an examination of all accessible authorities, is as positive as a careful mortal examination and judgment can be.

"Some bold attempts have lately been made to prove these [the
Casket] Letters and Sonnets to be forgeries ; but, unfortunately for
Mary's reputation, the principal arguments, in support of their authenticity, yet remain unanswered. 1. They were examined and compared
with her acknowledged handwriting, in many letters to Elizabeth, not
only by the English Commissioners, and by the Scottish Council and
Parliament, but by the English Privy Council, assisted by several noblemen well affected to the cause of the Queen of Scots, who all admitted
them to be authentic. (Anderson, Vol. IV.) This circumstance is of
great weight in the dispute ; for, although it is not very difficult to
counterfeit a subscription, ☞ it is almost impossible to counterfeit
any number of pages so perfectly as to elude detection. 2. Mary and
her commissioners, by declining to refute the charge of the Regent,
though requested to attempt a refutation in any manner or form, and
told by Elizabeth that silence would be considered as the fullest confes-
sion of guilt, seemed to admit the justice of the accusation. (*Id ibid.*) 3.
The Duke of Norfolk, who had been favored with every opportunity of

examining the letters in question, and who gave the strongest marks
of his attachment to the Queen of Scots, yet believed them to be
authentic. ("State Trials," Vol. I.) 4. In the conferences between the
Duke, Maitland of Lethington, and Bishop Lesley, all zealous partisans
of Mary, the authenticity of the letters, and her participation in the
murder of her husband, are always taken for granted. (*Id ibid.*) 5.
*But, independent of all other evidence, the letters themselves contain
many internal proofs of their authenticity ; many minute and unneces-
sary particulars, which could have occurred to no person employed to
forge them,* and which, as the English commissioners ingenuously observed, "were *unknown to any other than to herself and Bothwell.*"
6. *Their very indelicacy is a proof of their authenticity ;* for although
Mary, in an amorous moment, might slide into a gross expression,
☞ in writing to a man to whom she had sacrificed her honor, the
framer of no forgery could hope to gain it credibility by imputing such
expressions to so polite and accomplished a princess as the Queen of
Scots. (Vol. I., p. 462, note 2. "History of Modern Europe."   By
William Russell, LL. D.   Harper & Brothers, No. 82 Cliff Street, New
York. 1833.)

Note II. Did Mary have a child by Bothwell ?

Absolute proofs and circumstantial evidence accumulate to prove
that Mary Stuart had a child by Bothwell. Lord Mahon, a very careful
and trustworthy historian, in his Review of the "*Lettres, Instructions
et Memoires de Marie Stuart,*" &c., &c., by Prince Alexander Labanoff,
Article V., *Quarterly Review,* Vol. LXXVII., No. 153, London, 1846, page
139, &c., comes to the same conclusion as the Russian champion of the
Queen, that she did have a daughter by Bothwell. Labanoff says, Vol.
II., page 63, that this child was born in Lochleven Castle, in February,•
1568, exactly, or about, nine months after her third marriage, 15th
May, 1567.*

---

* 1567. 18th July. [Page 32.]—"The Lords of the Secret Council suggest to Mary
the disavowal of her marriage with Bothwell. She refuses—being unable to consent to
bastardize the infant of which she was then pregnant. See the letter from Throckmorton to Elizabeth, of 19th July, 1567. This letter, preserved in the British Museum
(Cotton Mss., Caligula C. I., fol. 18), has been printed by Robertson. Appendix, No.
XXII."   *   *   *
   1568.   [Page 34.]—"In February Mary is delivered of a daughter, at Lochleven ; the

Claude Nau, in his " History of Mary Stuart," edited by the Jesuit Joseph Stevenson, Edinburgh, 1883, pages 59-60, mentions her " lying on her bed, in a state of very great weakness, partly by reason of her great trouble (partly in consequence of a great flux, the result of a miscarriage of twins, her issue by Bothwell), so that she could move only with great difficulty."

This was the time that the miscreant Lindesay, the truculent Ruthven and Sir Robert Melville carried to Lochleven the Act of Abdication for Mary to sign. If Nau speaks the truth, and what reason had he for not doing so, the date must have been about 24th July, 1567. (Labanoff, II., 59.) Stevenson, in his lengthy Preface, pages clxxvii.-viii., a work in itself, is more explicit. These are his words, " Among the other revelations made to us by this [Nau's] narrative is one which takes us by surprise, the fact, namely, that shortly after her [Mary's] arrival in Lochleven, the Queen gave birth to twins, which, however, were still-born. Yet that such should have been the case might have been expected, for she herself declared that she was about to become a mother. Considering the rare intercourse which at this time took place between the ordinary household of the castle and the Queen's attendants, it is by no means incredible that the birth of these children was never known to the Laird of Lochleven and his family. It is never referred to in the correspondence of the period."

A note at the foot of the page, clxxvii., reads, " It must have occurred not long before 24th July " [1567]; that is in little more than two months

child is carried to France, where she eventually became a Nun in the Convent of our Lady at Soissons. The pregnancy of the Queen of Scotland has been denied by Gilbert Stuart, who wrote in 1782. But Dr. Lingard having reproduced this fact *as certain* in his 'History of England,' I have thought it right to adopt his account, supporting myself, moreover, by the testimony of Le Laboureur, an historian worthy of great credit, who, in his additions to the 'Memoirs of Castelnau' (Vol. I., p. 610, of the edition of 1731), speaks of the daughter of Mary Stuart. It must be remembered that the author whom I cite held an office of trust at the French court (he was the king's councillor and almoner), and that he had means of knowing several particulars long kept secret. Besides, when he published his work, it was easy for him to consult the registers of the Convent of our Lady at Soissons, and to assure himself if Mary's daughter had really been a nun there."—" Letters of Mary Stuart, Queen of Scotland, selected from the *Recuil des Lettres de Marie Stuart;* together with the Chronological Summary of Events during the Reign of the Queen of Scotland." By Prince Alexander Labanoff. Translated, with Notes and Introduction, by William Turnbull, Esq., Advocate, F. S. A. Scot. London : Charles Dolman, 61 New Bond Street. 1845.

after Mary and Bothwell were married, and justifies the argument of Prof. Schiern, that the marriage between Mary and Bothwell was precipitated in order to cover with the mantle of legitimacy, a child very likely the result of the double adultery of its parents.

Throckmorton, the English ambassador in Scotland, in a letter to Queen Elizabeth, under the date of 18th (19th) July, 1567, says, p. 142 : "She [Mary] hath sent me word that she will rather dye, grounding herself upon thys reason that takynge herself to be seven weeks gon with chylde, by renouncynge Bothwell, she should acknowledge herselfe to be with chylde of a bastard, and to have forfayted her honoure, which she will not do to dye for it."

Even an experienced and observant woman does not know that she is with child, so as to speak decidedly, until several, certainly two months have elapsed. Consequently this child dates back to before the double marriage rites, 15th May, 1567, to justify any idea that the twins (referred to by Nau and Stevenson) were boy and girl, because some writers refer to a girl, and some to a boy. If there was any child, only one, the sex, female, is undoubted, but the tradition of a son born to Mary, in Lochleven Castle, of which the paternity was assigned to George Douglas, is mentioned by Burton (IV., 864–5 ; VII., 82, 48, 49, 129, 185). As to the daughter, see de Peyster's "Mary Stuart, a Study," pp. 99–100. "Bothwell and Mary Stuart," 112–114, 196–198. Rapin, Lingard, Froude, Mignet, and others, contain references to a daughter, and Miss Yonge wrote a novel, "Unknown to History," founded on the birth and career of an unfortunate female child. The distinction between the sexes is not recognizable until after, at least, three or four months of life in the embryo, consequently the reasons urged by Prof. Schiern, why Mary was desirous of precipitating her marriage with Bothwell, is fully explained. Lord Mahon, Burton, and all of the writers who argue out these stories, do so like lawyers carrying conviction. The discrepancies in the statement of the birth of that child, or those children, seem to be founded, *not* on the facts of the case, but the feelings of the chroniclers. Agnes Strickland, wishing to blacken the character of Bothwell, and to clear Mary from all stain, makes her "painful and dangerous" illness at Lochleven "exactly nine months from the period" Bothwell is said to have ravished her in Dunbar Castle.

Prince Labanoff makes the birth occur in February, 1568, nine months after Mary's public marriage. Nau, Laboureur, Castelnau, Throckmorton : the first, her secretary ; the second, a priest of her communion ; the third, a friend and invariably admitted to have been an honest man ; and the fourth, a man who had nothing to gain by falsehood ; all agree us to the pregnancy or the birth of a child or twins. Nau and Stevenson make the date six months earlier than Miss Strickland, and seven than Labanoff. The only doubtful point is the survival of a child. It was no uncommon thing to place royal children who were annoyances in conventical establishments, in contradistinction to the course of other monarchs, such as James V. of Scotland, Henry IV. and Louis XIV. of France, Charles II. of England, and others, who amply provided for their bastards, and ennobled them. That Mary's child, if a girl, had a different fate, is not surprising. It was at once a menace to the parties in power, and a victim to the hatred universally exhibited towards its father, Bothwell, and its mother, Mary. In all ages, to make way with such a birth, is neither extraordinary nor even unusual. To have done justice to such an unhappy fruit of an anlawful union would have been a rare exception to a detestable rule, almost invariable in its application.

To quote at large from Lord Mahon's critical Review of Mary's Letters, &c., it states that " Prince Labanoff admits, " (Vol. II., p. 63,) "*without hesitation,* the statement that Queen Mary, when sent to the Castle of Lochleven, in June, 1567, was with child by Bothwell, and that in February, 1568, she gave birth to a daughter, who was immediately removed to France, and became a Nun at the convent of Notre Dame, at Soissons." Considering the marriage of Mary to Bothwell, 15th May, 1567, it is obvious that her character is in no way affected by this tale, whether true or false. On this point, therefore, Prince Labanoff's prepossessions in her favor have no force, and the judgment of so well-informed and laborious an inquirer deserves, as we think, the greatest weight. *His assent to this tale* has led us to inquire the grounds on which it rests ; and we shall now state what appear *the* testimonies in its favor, as well as the negative presumptions which may be raised against it. The statement rests mainly on the direct assertion of Le Laboureur, in his "Additions to the Memoires de Castelnau," and will be found at

Vol. I., p. 673, edition of 1659. Jean Le Laboureur (1562–75) is a writer
of great research and accuracy. He is described by M. Weiss, in the *Biographie Universelle* [compare *Biographie Generale*, XXX., *de Firmin
Didot and M. L. d'Hafer*], as " *l'un des écrivains qui ont le plus contribué
à éclaircir l'histoire de France.*" And as Prince Labanoff reminds us, he
held a post of high confidence at the Court of France (*Conseiller et Aum-
ónier du Roi*), and might become acquainted with many, until then very
secret, transactions. But, if we believe, as appears most probably the
case, that Le Laboureur derived the story from the manuscript notes
and papers left behind by Castelnau, the evidence in its favor will appear
stronger still. Michel de Castelnau, Seigneur de Mauvissiére (by which
latter name he was commonly known during his life), had accompanied
Mary, as French Ambassador to Scotland. In 1575 he was ap-
pointed French Ambassador in England; and, as appears from Prince
Labanoff's collection, became one of Mary's most frequent and most
trusted correspondents. Castelnau says in his Memoirs, "*Elle est en-
core prisonnière sans pouvoir trouver moyen d'en sortir qu'a l'instant
il ne survienne quelques nouvelles difficultiés, les quelles ont pour la
plupart passées par mes mains.*" (Vol. XXXIII., p. 357, in the collection
of Petitot.) It appears also that, in the course of his diplomatic and
political services, he had occasion to make many journeys through the
north of France, and he might *not improbably, in one of them, have
seen himself at Soissons, the unhappy offspring of a most ill-omened
and most guilty marriage.* There is, however, a remarkable *confirma-
tion* of Le Laboureur's story, wholly unknown to La Laboureur when
he wrote, and not published until a century afterwards. It is con-
tained in a secret dispatch from Throckmorton, the English Ambassador in Scotland, to his Queen, and will be found in the Appendix
to Robertson's History, under date of July 18th, 1567. It appears the
Ambassador had transmitted, by a secret channel, a proposal to Mary
at Lochleven, that she should renounce Bothwell for her husband. But
he adds, in his report to Elizabeth, " She hath sent me word that she
will rather dye, grounding herself upon thys reason, that takyne herself to be *seven weeks* [embryo, consequently, about two months old]
gon with chylde, by renouncynge Bothwell she should acknowledge
herself to be with chylde of a bastard, and to have forfayted her hon-

oure, which she will not do to dye for it." Physicians admit there
is uncertainty in the symptoms of pregnancy previous to the fifth
month, and, even later, the wisest and most observing are frequently
deceived. Consequently, to speak so positively, Mary must have had
more trustworthy evidence, and even this seems to establish Schiern's
views as well as those of Nau and Stevenson.

Nor can it, on examination of the circumstances, be maintained
that this answer was only a device of Mary to evade compliance. She
must have foreseen that, as really happened, the renouncing of Bothwell would be again and again pressed upon her, and that if her first
reason against it should, after some short interval, appear to be invalid
she would then be unable to take a stand on any other ground. The
concurrence of two such testimonies as Le Laboureur's in France and
Throckmorton's in Scotland—each entitled to high confidence and each
without the slightest knowledge of the other—would probably on most
questions *be considered as decisive.*

"In this case, however, we have to set against them a strong *primâ
facie* presumption on the other side—the utter silence as to this child
at Soissons in all the correspondence of the period—the utter silence,
first of Mary herself; secondly, of all her friends; and thirdly, of all
her opponents. We propose to consider, under each of these heads,
whether any sufficient ground for such silence can be assigned.

1. Mary herself had few opportunities of writing from her prison of
Lochleven. Even the industry of Prince Labanoff is compelled to leave
an utter blank between Sept. 3d, 1567, when Mary wrote to Sir Robert
Melville, desiring him to 'send stuffs for clothes for herself and my
maidens, for they are naked;' and March 31st, 1568, when we find two
notes, one to Catharine de Medici and the other to the Archbishop of
Glasgow, entreating speedy succor, and adding, *"je n'ose ecrire d'a-
vantage."* There are two other short notes from Lochleven, on the day
preceding her escape, one to Catherine de Medici, and one to Elizabeth.
In none of these could we expect to find any allusion to her pregnancy
or to the birth of her child.

There is no letter at all from Mary during the hurried fortnight
which elapsed between her escape from Lochleven and her arrival in
England, except a few lines of doubtful authenticity dated from

Dundrennan, and addressed to Queen Elizabeth, which we think Prince Labanoff has too hastily admitted. (The authority he cites for it is only "*Marie Stuart, Nouvelle Historique*," Paris, 1674. Moreover, the note from Dundrennan is not alluded to in the certainly authentic, letter which Mary addressed to Elizabeth from Workington only two days afterward.) This note, however, in no degree bears upon the present question. Within a very few weeks of her captivity in England, Mary became convinced of the horror with which her union with Bothwell was universally regarded. She consented, at the Conferences of York, that steps should be taken for the dissolution of her marriage and for the contracting of another with the Duke of Norfolk. From that time forward, therefore, we need not wonder that her letters should contain no allusion to the pledge of an alliance, which that pledge might, if known, render more difficult to dissolve, and which she knew was most hateful to all her well-wishers whether in France, in England, or in Scotland.

2. The same horror of this alliance and of its results may be thought an adequate motive for silence in such few of Mary's relatives or friends in France as must be supposed cognizant of the birth and existence of her daughter.

3. Of Mary's enemies, the first in power at this period was her illegitimate brother, the Earl of Murray, the Regent of Scotland. During a long time he professed a tender regard for his sister's reputation, and several times warned her against urging him to the public accusation which he made at last, on December 8th, 1568. It is, therefore, perfectly consistent with his professions and with his position that he should, in February, 1568, *have taken steps for the concealment of Mary's childbirth, and the sending of the infant to her relatives in France.* After December, 1568, there could no longer, indeed, be the slightest pretence to personal kindness and regard. But surely the chances of the royal succession would then supply him another and much stronger motive for concealment. In case the life of James VI. —a boy not yet three years old—should fail, Mary's daughter, if the marriage with Bothwell were legitimate, would become the next heir to the crown. A most perplexing question as to the strict validity of that marriage, and as to the rights of the true heir, would then arise.

It seems probable, therefore, in such a contingency, Murray and his associates in the secret had resolved to deny absolutely the fact of the birth or the existence of the infant.

The same motive for the greatest possible secrecy would have weight all through the life of the Nun at Soissons; but would cease at her death. And thus the same consideration would serve to explain both the silence observed during so many years, and the disclosure at last in Le Laboureur's annotation—always supposing the secret to have been confined, both in Scotland and in France, to extremely few and trusty persons.

We offer these conjectures as, in our mind, greatly diminishing, though not, we admit, entirely removing the force of the objections against the story. *And on the whole, looking to the positive testimonies in its favor, we certainly incline, with Prince Labanoff, to a belief in its* TRUTH. "

NOTE III. MARY AND KIRKALDY OF GRANGE.

The most careful analytical study of the character of Mary leads the unprejudiced critic, up or down, to the consistent judgment of the calm historian, Lord Mahon, "the strength of her passions ruined all;" hers " was an emotional nature, as ardent as it was unscrupulous." "Judicious calmness will not allow him [Burton, a fair and unprejudiced writer] to violate historic facts in order to impart a fictitious innocence to a sadly perverted and vitiated character." *"When she was not under the influence of the violent attachments to which she afterwards yielded* [1563–5]. Burton observes, in another place (IV., 95), "and while she views her marriage as a political arrangement, she scorned anything but a thoroughly great alliance." Yet she had been in love with Damville, and to him, in her favor, succeeded Chastelard, Sir John Gordon, and then the miserable Darnley. Every just critic will reject the imputation in regard to Rizzio, although it is very doubtful if he was the repulsive creature generally represented, but rather an insinuating, not unattractive man. "The beautiful Mary was, in reality, one of the most abandoned and unscrupulous of her sex." These are terrible extracts; each word seems to be wet with blood and stained with passion. Mary's conduct at Carberry Hill is utterly inexplicable, unless we accept as correct the definition of the arch-poet : "It [Love] is to be all made of *fantasy* " [" passion, wishes" or desires], said the arch-expression-dissector, "Love [such as that of Mary Stuart] is not altogether a delirium, yet it has many points in common therewith ;" and, remarks another celebrated critic, unless the idea of Burton is conceded as the true solution, "The latent resolution [of Kirkaldy to betray his party] was planted in his heart by the siren [Mary Stuart] when she chose to surrender to him [at Carberry Hill and abandon Bothwell to his fate]. She may have been carried away by a sudden flood of feeling, as she certainly was instantly captured by the exterior graces and accomplishments of Darnley. Finally, not to weary the reader with arguments, however powerful and pertinent, the question presents itself: Would Lindesay, "the bloodiest and most furious that could be found in the whole troop" (Stevenson, clxxix.), if he did not believe that he had guaged her nature, have dared to make her the proposition, in Lochleven Castle, that "he would free her if she would love him ?" (Nau, 59.)

Lindesay afterward became one of her partisans. She was a veritable Circe. Again, would Ruthven have dared to commit a like offense without some excuse ? "Ruthven, who had been commissioned to reside within the [Lochleven] Castle [with Lindesay] as her keepers," " was removed in consequence of having been guilty of an act of scandalous indecency. Early one morning he came into the bedroom of his captive and made indecent proposals to her ; offering to procure her liberty at the payment of her sin." (Stevenson, clxxviii.)

Ruthven, like Lindesay, afterward joined her party (Nau, 59). These relations tally with the curious story told by Michelet of Margaret of Valois, another royal lady of peculiar temperament and passionate nature.

Margaret of Valois had innumerable lovers, and especially her brothers, the King, Henry III., and the Duke of Alencon, a candidate for the hand of Elizabeth of England. Henry III., who survived her, was not less jealous of her ; was more husband than her real husband, the spiritual and patient King of Navarre, afterwards Henry IV. Margaret's lover, for the time being, was the famous duelist, Bussy of Amboise, of whom the king's favorite du Guast was at once accuser, or informer and persecutor. On the 30th of October, 1575, Margaret de-

termined upon a decided step, and demonstrated that she was the true
sister of the King, Charles IX., the hero of St. Bartholomew's day. She
looked up an assassin. In the Convent of the Augustins, a certain
Baron of Viteaux was in hiding, who had killed, among others, one of
the immediate circle of Henry III. Had it not been for du Guast, this
king who had a short memory could have been easily worked upon to
pardon Viteaux. Consequently Viteaux detested du Guast. Margaret did not hesitate to seek out this man of blood, either in the
cloister, or more probably the vast and dark church in which he kept
himself concealed. This was in the night before All Souls Day, and
the occasion was favorable. All the church bells of the capital were
clanging in chorus, and the Parisians having passed the whole day in
frequenting churches and visiting tombs, had sought their homes
early. Margaret availed herself of these circumstances, so opportune
to her occasion. Trembling and shuddering, she asked Viteaux to do
for her sake that which he himself desired to do for his own. Viteaux
nevertheless, fought shy, and did not wish to do the deed gratis : if
tradition is reliable. She promised ; he required immediate settlement.
It was night, and all the numerous dead, in this church full of sepulchres,
awaiting their annual festival, were not more peaceable and uncon-
cerned than the sleeping living. The intrepid little woman paid cash
down. Her man kept his bargain : du Guast was killed the next day.
(Michelet, X., V., 82.)

Ruthven expected the same sort of pay, but Mary did not see it in
the same light as Margaret. Perhaps she did not trust her Scotchman
and did not believe he would or could carry out the contract.

NOTE IV. MAITLAND OF LETHINGTON.

"Thenceforward, therefore, we see a double current where before
there had been but a single stream. Murray became the head of the religious party ; Maitland of Lethington of the political ; and the distinction of the ends which they proposed to themselves soon widened the
separation between them.

"Maitland, *who cared as much for religion as politicians are usually
apt to care*, discovered in the disputed title of Elizabeth to her crown,
and in the right to it which had been advanced for his own Queen, an

opportunity of re-establishing Scotland on its old equality with its old rival, and perhaps for a splendid repayment of old scores and grudges. Intrigue was his proper element. Life was a game in which he was mainly interested as an exercise of political ability, and the 'situation' had irresistible attractions for him. No sooner was Mary returned than she found in him the most efficient minister of her ambition. He threw himself into all her schemes, and gave them shape and consistency ; and in a few years he had sown the seeds of disaffection over the whole northern counties of England. He parried Elizabeth's demand for a ratification of the Treaty of Edinburgh (in which it had been stipulated that Mary should formally renounce her claim) by a counter-demand that she should be acknowledged as her successor ; and Elizabeth's refusal, which the circumstances of the case rendered inevitable, he was able to display as a national affront in the eyes of the proud and foolish nobility. Everything prospered with him. A dexterous flattery had dissolved the Protestant League ; Murray was almost the only nobleman who openly adhered to it ; and in the atmosphere of suspicion which Maitland had contrived to create, a coldness had arisen even towards Murray among the ministers of the Kirk. The Darnley marriage was probably Maitland's devising ; for Mary's title was doubly fortified by it, and at once upon its taking place a large section of the English transferred their allegiance to her. The northern counties were ready to rise in the summer of 1565, and the attempt would not long have been delayed if Darnley's own wretched character had not ruined everything. No one could trust him, and yet it was impossible to act without him ; and at the end of a year, it was found indispensably necessary, unless their entire policy was to fall in pieces, that in some way or other he should be got rid of. Maitland was the first person who suggested the Murder to the Queen ; and if she could have left it to him as he desired, the thing would have been done skillfully and quietly, and Darnley would have disappeared out of life with as little disturbance as a thousand other poor princes had caused in disappearing who have been in the way of politicians. Maitland had been responsible for his introduction upon the stage, and like a good subject he was ready to do his best to remedy the evil which he had caused. *Disappointment is a feeble word for the feeling with which he must have regarded the sub-*

stitution of Bothwell for himself, and the sacrifice of an empire for a miserable love intrigue. Everything was ruined irretrievably; and, although, even after Carberry Hill, *Maitland undertook if she would promise to surrender Bothwell, to restore her Crown, yet her refusal convinced him that her cause was for the time hopeless,* and he consented with the rest of the nobles to her deposition and imprisonment in Lochleven. She had committed herself in every way; even on paper; in letters of her own handwriting; and though such men as Maitland find little difficulty in forgiving crimes, blunders, gross patent blunders, are without excuse. Accordingly, as long as she remained in Scotland, he now kept himself comparatively in the background, doing little or nothing, but formally acting with his old friends, and supporting Murray. In the autumn of 1568, however, a new complication brought around fresh opportunities, and the old hopes grew green again. Murray's regency was secretly detestable to him—a very solecism in government, unendurable by a philosophical statesman. As long as it lasted the moral law was the law of the land. Sins were punished as crimes, and political difficulties were resolved by a stupid and unstatesmanlike appeal to the 'Word of God.' *Such a state of things was an affront to his very creed, and an outrage on his understanding.* Self preservation is the first law of life; and if theories such as these obtained currency what would be the use of the Maitlands? His national pride was further irritated at the position in which Mary had been placed by Elizabeth, who had compelled her to plead at an English tribunal; his jealousy was alarmed by the evident anxiety of the English Government to get the young King into their hands; and Mary herself was now in a country where the evidence of her guilt was less notorious, and where it was possible to deny it. Bothwell was safe out of the way in a Danish prison, and she immediately on her arrival in England had been welcomed by a powerful party, who were secretly ready to recognise her as the representative of the Catholic cause. All these things combined to revive the old schemes; and Murray, when summoned to York to meet the English commissioners, had already seen so much cause to distrust Maitland that he was afraid to leave him behind and had joined him with himself in the commission.

"Perhaps he had already been in secret correspondence with Mary; at any rate, he was no sooner in York, than he placed himself in correspondence with her, and privately directed her in the course which she was to pursue in defending herself. But the worst mischief which Maitland could have done in Scotland was small in comparison with that which his visit to England gave him the opportunity of effecting. Whatever admiration is due to audacity and skill must be given him without stint for the scheme which he now conceived. The Duke of Norfolk, who had been sent to York as the President of the English commission, was the first English subject, the premier nobleman in the peerage. Professing himself to be a Protestant, his allegiance to the Reformation was as hollow as that of the mass of the nobility. If Mary Stuart could be married to *him*, and if he would support her title to the crown, her success, Maitland considered, would be certain.   *   *   *

"It was a really magnificent scheme. Although it failed, there is something grand even in failure on such a scale; and Maitland must have the credit as well as the responsibility of the entire conception."

Fraser's Magazine, Vol. 42, p. 537-8.

www.ingramcontent.com/pod-product-compliance
Lightning Source LLC
Chambersburg PA
CBHW032201010726
47493CB00008BA/2779